Goosebumps

THE HAUNTING RETURNS

Goosebumps

THE HAUNTING RETURNS

BASED ON THE SCHOLASTIC BOOK SERIES BY R.L. STINE

KATE HOWARD

Scholastic Inc.

Copyright © 2024 Scholastic Inc.™ & © Scholastic Inc. SCHOLASTIC, GOOSEBUMPS, and associated logos are trademarks and/or registered marks of Scholastic Inc. All rights reserved.

All rights reserved. Published by Scholastic Inc., *Publishers since 1920*. SCHOLASTIC and associated logos are trademarks and/or registered trademarks of Scholastic Inc.

The publisher does not have any control over and does not assume any responsibility for author or third-party websites or their content.

No part of this publication may be reproduced, stored in a retrieval system, or transmitted in any form or by any means, electronic, mechanical, photocopying, recording, or otherwise, or used to train any artificial intelligence technologies, without written permission of the publisher. For information regarding permission, write to Scholastic Inc., Attention: Permissions Department, 557 Broadway, New York, NY 10012.

This book is a work of fiction. Names, characters, places, and incidents are either the product of the author's imagination or are used fictitiously, and any resemblance to actual persons, living or dead, business establishments, events, or locales is entirely coincidental.

ISBN 978-1-5461-5431-0

10 9 8 7 6 5 4 3 2 1   24 25 26 27 28

Printed in the U.S.A. 40
First printing 2024

Book design by Jeff Shake

Goosebumps

THE HAUNTING RETURNS

BEFORE

— *1993* —

HAROLD
BIDDLE

PROLOGUE

*R*ain drenched the town of Port Lawrence. The gray skies matched the pallor of Harold Biddle's sallow skin. Harold kicked puddles as he walked home alone from the high school, looking forward to the one thing he enjoyed each day: spending his free time in the basement of his wooded house, photographing the treasures he'd collected.

As he slogged through the classic Pacific Northwest afternoon, Harold spotted something writhing in the mud outside the old hunting shack he called home. He bent down and plucked a lone earthworm off the ground, tucking it into his pocket to add to his collection of pets.

When he passed through the kitchen, Harold grabbed a packet of hot chocolate powder out of the cupboard and ripped it open, tossing the contents back for a quick afternoon snack. He was home alone—again.

Before trudging down to his basement lair, Harold stopped to snap a picture of the cuckoo clock at the top of the stairs, just as the bird poked its head out of the clock to announce the time. When Harold got downstairs, he tossed his backpack on his desk, alongside his paints, brushes, and projects in process. Digging into his pocket, Harold pulled out the worm he found on the ground outside and dumped it into a glass terrarium alongside all the other worms—his friends. His parents had never approved of his pets. They thought his choice of worms would make him seem weird to other kids. But Harold loved them and found comfort in his collection.

He grabbed his camera again and snapped a picture of his new pet nestled in with the group.

With a wry half-smile, Harold dumped the photo on the desk beside a scrapbook filled with his drawings, collages, poetry, and photographs. He leaned in to study his latest masterpiece—a mask he'd been working on—and took another photo.

The doorbell rang upstairs, and Harold startled, snapping his head up. Visitors weren't common at the Biddle house, and they weren't exactly welcome. Harold didn't have many friends, so anyone who'd stop by probably wasn't there to hang out and watch TV. Slowly, he made his way up the stairs and dragged open the wooden front door. There was no one on the porch.

Closing the door behind him, Harold took a step back toward the basement stairs, and then the doorbell rang again. This time, Harold couldn't pretend it hadn't sounded. There was undoubtedly someone out there, someone ringing the bell. He opened the door again and stepped out onto the front porch, taking a cautious step into the now-dark evening. "Hello?" Something rustled behind him, so Harold spun around—but found nothing. His breath quickened; he quickly stepped inside to escape the night.

Just as he reached out to pull the front door closed again, it slammed shut on its own. Harold felt something nearby—a presence of some sort—but nothing was there. Nothing he could see, anyway. A vase suddenly crashed to the floor next to him, and Harold spun in a panicked circle.

"Who's there?" he screamed, his eyes wide and searching.

The lights flickered. A lamp tipped over in front of him. Books began to pour off the living room's built-in shelves. And then the house went black.

Harold gasped as terror gripped him from every side. Running his hand along the wall, he stumbled toward the fireplace at the other end of the living room. He reached for a match, then held it out to light a candle— it was enough to give him some light, some comfort. Using the candlelight to guide him, Harold hustled toward the basement—the only place he ever felt safe and strong.

The cuckoo clock began to chirp on repeat. Over and over, the clock droned—cuckoo, cuckoo, cuckoo. Slamming the basement door to shut out the sound of the obviously broken clock, Harold stumbled onto the top stair, locking the door behind him. Something or someone pounded at the door, and Harold gasped. "Stay away from me!" he screamed. Above him, the house was suddenly alive with noises—footsteps, slamming cabinets, that awful cuckoo clock on its endless loop.

In a panic, Harold tripped and fell down the stairs. The candle arced out of his hand, landing alongside Harold on the old, dry basement carpet at the bottom of the steps. In an instant, the fire caught. As Harold screamed and beat at the floor to try to stop the fire from spreading, the flames took hold and gobbled everything up . . . including Harold Biddle.

PART ONE

— *Isaiah* —

SAY CHEESE
AND DIE!

CHAPTER ONE

"Morning, Nora!" Sixteen-year-old Isaiah Howard sidled up to the counter of the Harbor Stop, Port Lawrence's dockside general store and café. "Can I have a bacon burrito? And one of those waffle things."

"Nice." Isaiah's best friend, James, nodded. "Love those."

"Then order your own waffle thing," Isaiah said, nudging his friend in the ribs. "I don't want you grabbing at my food."

"Guys," the shop's owner, Nora, began. Nora had known these two their whole lives. Not only had she gone to school with Isaiah's dad and James's mom, but she also had a son, Lucas, who went to high school with the two friends.

James jumped in before Nora could say her piece. "Another waffle thing. And whatever your most colorful cereal is. Two of those."

"Guys," Nora said again, holding out a hand. "The credit card machine is down today. Cash only."

"But we're living in a cashless society!" James protested. He thrust out his lower lip, groaning at the injustice. Whether it was fashion, cars, snacks, or clothes, James wasn't accustomed to being told no. Though his style screamed casual and artsy—cardigan, perfect pearls, and a slouchy pair of pants that made his legs look *amazing*—it cost a small fortune to perfect that look.

"No food?" Isaiah wailed. As a muscled athlete, Isaiah was always hungry. He tried out his killer smile, hoping the Isaiah charm would have the desired effect. "But we're starving."

"Feed the needy!" James wheedled, flipping his curly bangs away from his eyes.

"You are not needy," Nora said, leveling him with a look. "Your car is bigger than my apartment."

Isaiah pouted. Like James, he also wasn't used to not getting what he wanted. He was the star quarterback, after all, and that title came with a certain set of perks. "But we're hungry. So hungry."

"You're really going to deny us a second breakfast?" James whined.

"Second breakfast?" Nora said with a dry laugh. After a moment, she relented—and gave them each a packet of crackers. "Knock yourselves out."

James frowned at the crumbly crackers inside a sad plastic wrapper. "I didn't know people actually ate these."

"Yeah," Isaiah said, scoffing. "I thought they were something that came free with soup."

Nora smirked. "They are."

As the two friends headed toward James's fully loaded Jeep Wrangler, Nora's son, Lucas, called out from somewhere within the parking lot. "Watch your backs!"

James and Isaiah spun around just in time to see Lucas come zipping off the edge of the café's roof astride his skateboard. He face-planted on the concrete below, then looked up at the other two with a bloody smile and said, "I'm good."

"Lucas!" Nora screamed from inside the shop. "I told you to stop doing that!"

"It's cool, Mom," Lucas said, spitting blood. "It's just my head this time."

"I get really nervous around him," James said as he climbed into the Jeep,

"Bro, how is this man still alive?" Isaiah asked.

CHAPTER TWO

"All right," Coach Rifkin cheered at the center of the high school gym. The stands at the pep rally were packed with students there to support the school's football team before their big game that weekend. "Let's give it up for our Port Lawrence Titans and their team captain and my favorite person"—Coach cut off with a laugh, then continued—"wasn't supposed to say that, but I just did—Isaiah Howard!"

Isaiah ran onto center court. "Port Lawrence High!" he screamed into the mic. "How y'all doin'?" The crowd filling the gym cheered. "Port Lawrence High, this is our *year*! This is our *time*! The glory days are right at our fingertips. Hold 'em up—hold up your glory fingertips!"

The whole room followed Isaiah's lead, wriggling their fingertips in the air.

"I love this town!" Isaiah screamed to even bigger cheers. "I love this game! But most importantly . . . I love you guys!"

Meanwhile, in the back corner of the gym's bleachers, Margot Stokes turned the page of her book and tried to tune out the pep rally. One side of her chin-length brown hair swung away from her ear and covered her face, creating a perfect shield from the rest of the gym. Her dad, Colin—the school's guidance counselor—sidled up and slid into the open spot beside her. "Hey, honey," he said.

"Dad." Margot gave him a withering look (an expression mastered by all high school geniuses).

"Sorry," Colin said, holding up his hands innocently. "Forgot we're at school, so you're not my daughter. Hello, Margot. Did you bring a *book* to a pep rally?"

Margot slammed the cover shut and sighed. "This is my way of hiding my lack of school spirit. Did it work?" In some ways, Margot wished she could fit in with everyone else at school a little better, but when she witnessed the idiocy surrounding her at events like pep rallies, she was glad she *didn't* fit in. She'd prefer being labeled a preppy nerd to being called a fashionable idiot any day.

"No," Colin said with a shake of his head. "It did not." He suddenly noticed the school's mascot—a titan, played by James—was making lewd gestures at center court. "James!" he called out, waving his hands to get the mascot to stop. "We've discussed this!" Colin marched off to have a word with the mascot.

With Margot's dad gone, Lucas took his chance to slide into the open seat next to her. "Football players suck," he said, rolling his eyes. As usual, his jeans were ripped, his hoodie somehow *wrinkled*, and his curly dark hair was a mess. He had a collection of cuts and scrapes decorating his face and arms from all his reckless skateboarding and biking accidents. Margot lifted her eyebrows and gazed at him through her glasses. She didn't actually hate football players; she just hated the whole "school spirit around football and football alone" thing. Lucas cringed, getting the message that Margot didn't agree. He'd been trying to impress her for years and had yet to succeed. He sighed. "That was insensitive. Sorry. They don't actually suck. No one sucks. Everyone's got their stuff."

"No one sucks?" Margot asked him, her lip quirking up into a teasing smile. "You stand by that? So, Jeffery Dahmer, he's a cool dude?" She raised her eyebrows. "Andrew Johnson? He's a chiller?"

Lucas shrugged, grinning like a dumb puppy. "I don't know who that is, but I gotta trust you."

Back in the center of the gym, Isaiah was still pumping up the crowd. "On three!" he screamed. "One . . . two . . . three . . . TITANS!" Then he held out his hand, dangling the mic over the hard gym floor.

Nearby, Isabella was filming the pep rally for the AV club. She watched as Isaiah wrapped up another Isaiah show. "Please don't drop the superexpensive mic," she muttered, fully aware that he wouldn't hear her. No one ever did.

Isaiah dropped the mic. It landed with a clatter just as his perky girlfriend, Allison, rushed toward him to help celebrate. Isabella raced over to pick the microphone up from the floor, and Isaiah pointed at her. "Hey, thanks, Susan!"

Isabella glared at his retreating back. Ten years going to school together and that's the best he could do? *Susan*? "It's Isabella," she said, but Isaiah was already gone.

CHAPTER THREE

"Whoa," James said, holding out a hand to stop Isaiah as they made their way down the crowded hallway later that day. He peeked over his best friend's shoulder as he spotted his crush, by far the most epically hot guy at school. "It's Sam. Be cool. Be cool."

"What does that mean?" Isaiah asked. "Be cool? What are we doing? I need more specific instructions."

"'Sup," James said, lifting his chin at Sam.

Sam glanced back at him and lifted an eyebrow. "'Sup." James's stomach flipped nervously. This was *progress*.

From behind James, Isaiah popped up on his toes and shouted out, "'Sup."

As soon as Sam was gone, James spun around to glare at his best friend. "What the hell was that?"

"I don't know," Isaiah said, wide-eyed. "I thought we were all saying hi to each other."

"No, that was a very delicate moment," James said with a deep breath. "We were a solid five steps away from something substantial I can tell my therapist about."

"You didn't give me any direction!" Isaiah groaned.

Just then, Allison sidled up behind Isaiah and came in for a kiss. "Hey, babe."

Isaiah turned to Allison and said, "James still hasn't asked Sam out."

"What's taking you so long?" Allison asked, looping her arm through Isaiah's. Tall, perfectly dressed, and drop-dead gorgeous, Allison could make anyone look good just by standing beside them. She and Isaiah were the It Couple at school, and they both knew—and loved—it.

"Why are you all up in my business?" James snapped back.

"Because we love you," Allison said at the same time Isaiah answered, "Boredom."

Allison's phone buzzed in her hand. She glanced down and groaned. On-screen, the video invite to her Halloween party was playing—but someone had altered it to make Allison sound like a pig. "That person who's been trolling me altered my invite." She held the phone out so the other two could watch with her. "How bad is it?"

James cringed. "A thousand views this morning. Yikes."

"It's just so annoying," Allison said. "It's clearly someone at school. I'm not mean to anyone. I'm literally super nice. Why am I getting trolled?"

"I know, right?" James said, nodding. "By the way, is Sam coming to your party?"

"Really?" Allison asked. "You're just changing the subject back to you?"

"Yeah, people do crazy things when they're in love." James grinned at her.

Colin popped his head out of his office and called out, "Isaiah, quick word?"

Allison and James took off while Isaiah jogged over to the guidance counselor, who also happened to be his neighbor. "What's up, Mr. Stokes?"

"Look, I don't want to be a bummer," Colin said, inviting Isaiah to take a seat in his office. "But you landed on academic probation and can't play on Friday."

Isaiah laughed, but then realized Mr. Stokes wasn't joking. "Wait, what? No! I have to. There are going to be scouts at that game."

"I know," Colin said, trying to calm him down. "I already spoke to Ms. Dowling. She says all you have to do is get an A on the big history test tomorrow, and she'll take you off probation."

"There's a history test tomorrow?" Isaiah replied. He was dumbstruck. This game was everything. His only chance at college was getting a football scholarship. He *had* to play in the game, or his future was shot. His family needed this.

"Hilarious." Colin laughed, assuming he was kidding. "Just get the A, and everything will be fine. Remember, we're all counting on you!"

Great, Isaiah thought, hanging his head. *No pressure.*

CHAPTER FOUR

The Biddle house had stood empty for thirty years. Ever since teenage Harold's death by fire in 1993, the place had been abandoned, left to rot.

Until now.

Nathan Bratt rolled into the driveway of his new woodland home, drinking it in. It was all his. He couldn't believe he'd inherited a place like this. He wandered around the front of the property, checking it out. The place was a bit of a dump, but with help from the contractor he'd hired, he'd turn it into a home. Carpenters swarmed around outside the house, fixing things to get the place ready for him to move in—finally.

Inside, he spotted someone hard at work, fixing something inside the fireplace. "Boo!" Nathan called out as a greeting.

Ben Howard, Isaiah's dad, jerked up—hitting his head on the fireplace in the process. "Ah, crap!" Ben said, rubbing his head.

"Oh my god, I'm so sorry," Nathan said, cringing. He hadn't meant to hurt the guy—he'd thought it was funny. "That backfired. I'm Nathan Bratt, the new owner."

"Ben Howard," Ben said, extending his hand to shake. "Nice to finally meet you. Sorry it's taking so long to get this place back together."

"It's okay. The house has been sitting empty for thirty years," Nathan said, waving him off. "I get it."

"We're not doing much more than getting the basics working," Ben said.

"Whatever makes it livable," Nathan said. He didn't care what shape the place was in—as long as the important stuff worked. It was *a* place to live, which was more than he'd had before.

"So, you inherited the house?" Ben asked, following Nathan as he wandered around the living room.

"Yeah," Nathan said with a shrug. "Turns out I'm the closest living relative. Never thought I'd be a homeowner on my salary." He wandered toward a door at the far end of the living room and gestured to it. "Where's that go?"

Ben sighed. "Basement. You know what happened down there, right?"

"Yeah, the lawyer filled me in," Nathan said, frowning. "Pretty gross. He said the parents disappeared after the kid burned to death. You know what that means, right?"

"What?"

"The parents did it," Nathan said simply. "It's always the parents." He eyed the door. "Can I go down there and check it out?"

Ben shook his head. "The door is stuck. Won't budge. Even if I could get it open, there's probably so much damage I couldn't get it up to code. Better if you just let me panel over it. Make like it's not there."

Nathan reached out a hand and tried the door handle. "I at

least want to see what's down there first." He picked up a crowbar and gestured toward the door. "Mind if I . . . ?"

Ben shrugged and watched as Nathan tried to pry open the door. It was clearly very stuck. But Nathan wasn't giving up. He jammed the crowbar into the frame harder and pried again. This time, the crowbar popped out and sliced open Nathan's hand. Blood immediately began to drip onto the wooden floorboards.

Nathan swore, clutching his wounded hand to his chest as the crowbar clattered to the ground at his feet.

"You need stitches," Ben said, checking out the new home-owner's hand. "I'll drive you."

As Nathan and Ben walked out, leaving the house shrouded in empty silence once again, the blood from Nathan's hand that had pooled on the floor made its move, too. It ran across the floorboards, then crawled up the locked basement door and sunk into the thirsty wooden panel. As soon as the blood had all been absorbed, the lock clicked—and the basement door slowly creaked open on its own, ready to welcome a new generation.

CHAPTER FIVE

Later that day, Isaiah sat on the old swing in his backyard, feeling hopeless. He'd spent most of the afternoon listening to his parents fight—about him and his football scholarship, as always.

"You okay?" Margot asked through the fence between her house and the Howards'. Though they didn't talk at school, and they couldn't be more different when looking at their lives from the outside, she and Isaiah had actually been friends forever—and she could always tell when something was wrong with her onetime best friend.

"I'm fine," Isaiah replied, trying to play it off.

"No, you're not," Margot said, strolling over to sit beside him. "You're doing your Isaiah face."

"What's 'Isaiah face'?" he asked with a smirk.

Margot did her best impression, saying, "Hey, I'm Isaiah, and everything is cool, 'cause I'm cool, cool, cool." Isaiah grinned. He knew Margot had read him like one of her books. "I could hear your parents fighting from my window. It's not fair to you how much they have riding on your football career."

"Doesn't matter," Isaiah said, hanging his head. "I can't play, anyway."

"What are you talking about?"

Isaiah groaned. "If I don't get an A on tomorrow's history

test, I sit out the game. Then I'm no good to anybody. Football's all I got."

"Football isn't all you got." Margot leveled him with a serious look. "You're excellent at eating hot dogs. You have a shoebox full of Pokémon cards that you really should have gotten rid of by now. And when you sing in the shower, you're not afraid to let the whole neighborhood know you're tone-deaf."

Isaiah couldn't help but smile. But then his mood fell again. "I'm serious, Margot." He knew he had to play in that game. Without football, he was nothing.

"Hey, this is not a big deal," Margot said, leaning into him. "All you have to do is get an A on the test. How much of the Constitution have you read?"

Isaiah squinted. "I listened to most of *Hamilton*."

"*Not* the Constitution," Margot noted.

Isaiah suddenly brightened. "Hey, what if you help me?"

"Like, study? That could be fun—"

Isaiah cut her off with a laugh. "No, nerd. Like, show me your answers."

"You mean cheat."

"Call it whatever you want." Isaiah shrugged.

"I just did," Margot spat back. "It's cheating."

"Please, Margot," Isaiah begged.

Margot glared back at him, but eventually his heartbroken look broke her down. "Just this once."

"Yes!" Isaiah said, pumping his fist. "Thank you so much!"

Margot grinned despite the fact that she'd just agreed to *cheat* on a test. If she could help out Isaiah, just this one time, it was worth it to keep him eligible for the big game. He deserved a shot. "You owe me."

The next day, Margot and Isaiah put their plan in action. Margot leaned left throughout the test, so Isaiah could copy every single one of her answers. As they walked out of the classroom after the test, Margot was all fired up. "That was so dangerous!" she said, grinning at Isaiah. "But also, like, such a rush! I'm gonna journal the hell out of this."

"Please don't put our crime in writing." Isaiah grinned back at her. "By the way, how do you think we did?"

"A, of course. You're playing that game."

"Thank you, Margot!" Isaiah said, shooting her a huge smile. He knew how much this meant, for her to cheat—for him.

As they made their way down the hall, Margot asked, "Hey, after school do you wanna—"

But before she could finish her thought, Allison ran up to them, obviously upset. "I'm screwed!" she wailed. "That stupid troll leaked my Halloween party plan to my *parents* on their vacation—tagged, DMed, *and* emailed them." She groaned. "Who does that? Who hates me that much? Mom forced me to delete the post. I have to cancel the party."

Isaiah considered this for a moment. "No, you don't." There had to be a way around this; there was a work-around for everything. He brightened as he got an idea. "You just need a new venue."

CHAPTER SIX

"Is this good enough for you?" Isaiah asked with a grin as James drove him and Allison up the long driveway leading to the old Biddle estate. Nothing had *ever* been a more perfect venue for a Halloween party than this creepy old house that was shrouded in mystery.

"It's *so* good," Allison said.

"I can't believe we're going to party at the Biddle house!" James whispered as they all crept up to the door.

Isaiah snapped open the lock box his dad had attached to the front door so the construction crew could get in. Luckily, his dad used the same code for everything, so it was easy to guess. He jangled the house keys in the air, then bent down to slide one into the lock. "New owner doesn't move in until tomorrow." He led his friends through the front door and into the house.

"Whoa," James mused, taking it all in. The old Biddle place was creepy, no doubt. "This is worth losing your father's trust over."

Isaiah laughed. It was all good. No one would ever need to know about this. He slipped off his shirt and threw on the long blond wig he had brought along as his costume. Spinning around, he revealed his look to his girlfriend and best friend.

"What are you supposed to be?" James blurted out. "A romance novel cover?"

Isaiah frowned. "No." He posed, waiting for them to figure it out.

"You're just shirtless. You just forgot a shirt," James pointed out.

Isaiah held up his mallet and pointed to his wig. "I'm Thor."

Allison frowned. "Why is Thor wearing cargo pants?"

"You hate it," Isaiah said, tugging off the wig and throwing his sweatshirt back on. "Forget about it."

As Isaiah and James began to set up, plugging in their speakers, fog machine, and party lights, Allison wandered around the first floor of the Biddle house, taking everything in. "Where did that kid die again?" she asked, rubbing her arms with her hands. The place was undoubtedly creepy.

"In the basement," Isaiah answered. "It caught on fire, and he got trapped inside."

"Like my bagel this morning," James mused.

"Maybe this wasn't such a good idea," Allison said. "What if this place is haunted?"

"Then it's the perfect party house on Halloween," Isaiah said with a grin, flicking a switch to turn on all their stuff. With a loud *pop!* all the lights went out.

"Party's over?" James suggested.

All three of them flicked on their phone flashlights. "Probably a tripped breaker," Isaiah explained. "Easy to fix if we can find the box." Suddenly, the basement door swung open with a loud creak. He glanced at James, then began to walk toward the open door. "Did you see that?"

James groaned. "Oh, cool, let's walk toward the creepy sound."
Isaiah continued walking. "I was being sarcastic. Hey, yo—" James
rushed after him; *together* was better than *alone* in a probably
haunted house.

"I bet the fuse box is down there," Isaiah said, peering down
the stairway. The space was narrow, and the old stairs led down to
solid blackness at the bottom.

"Yeah," James squeaked. "Probably just a few feet away from
where that kid was burned alive."

"Hey." A sudden voice behind them made all three of them
jump and spin around. "What are you guys doing?"

"Margot?" Isaiah asked, squinting to be sure he wasn't seeing
things in the black gloom of the house.

"What are *you* doing here?" Allison asked.

"I was invited," Margot said.

"By *who*?" Allison asked, her voice sharp.

Margot glanced at Isaiah, who looked back at her blankly. But
suddenly, he remembered. "Oh! Me. I mean, yeah—I invited
Margot." He turned to his girlfriend, who was giving him a death
stare. "I mean, everyone was invited, right?"

"I thought the party started at eight," Margot said, checking
the time on her phone. "Where is everyone?"

"Everyone usually shows up an hour late," Allison told her, arms
folded over her chest. "Sorry if that wasn't clearer on your invite."

"Let's just get the lights back on," Isaiah said, trying to break
some of the tension between the girls. "Who's going down there
with me?"

"No way," Allison said, taking a step back.

"I'll go with you," Margot offered.

Allison shook her head and glared at Margot. "Uh, no."

"You guys stay here," Isaiah said. There was no way he was gonna face Allison's wrath if he and Margot went down into the creepy basement together. His girlfriend was awesome, but she was also very much the jealous type. And he and Margot . . . well, they had history. As *friends*, nothing more, but it was still history nonetheless. "James will go with me."

"Yeah, no," James said, taking a step backward. "James is staying up here, too."

With a sigh, Isaiah headed down the stairs—alone. "Okay, Isaiah," he said softly, trying to calm his nerves. Each step down to the basement groaned under his weight. "It's just a basement." At the bottom, Isaiah shone his phone light around to get his first look at the charred space. He took in Harold's ancient computer, an old glass tank, and an old-school Polaroid camera. Then his phone light trailed past the desk and illuminated a white, pasty face, glaring back at him from within the basement doom.

CHAPTER SEVEN

A t the top of the stairs, the door to the basement slammed shut. "Not funny, James," Allison said. "Open the door."

James spun around. "I didn't shut it."

All three of them began to pound on the door and tug on the handle—but the door wouldn't budge. "What if Isaiah is hurt down there?" Allison wailed.

With one final tug at the doorknob, James lost his grip and slammed backward against the wall. His head cracked against the old cuckoo clock, knocking something loose, which caused the clock to begin to tick again after decades of silence. The bird leaped out of its house and began to chime—*cuckoo, cuckoo, cuckoo*. James rubbed his head and wobbled back to standing.

The basement door suddenly swung open a crack, and all three of them could hear something creaking up the dark stairs. "Isaiah?" Allison called out nervously.

There was a bright flash, then the door burst fully open. "Say cheese!" Isaiah called, pointing an old Polaroid camera right at Allison's terrified face.

"That's not funny!" Allison said, shoving him.

"You didn't see your face." Isaiah laughed.

Allison grabbed the Polaroid from Isaiah and shook it. "Where's the picture?"

"Smile!" Isaiah lifted the camera and took a picture of Margot while Allison continued to wait for the first image to appear. Suddenly, the lights and music flicked back on again.

"You found the fuse box?" Margot asked.

"Uh . . ." Isaiah replied, confused. "No. It wasn't down there."

"Whatever," Allison said, heading back to the living room. "It works now. Tonight is gonna be fun. I'm willing the fun into being. Let's finish setting up before everyone gets here!"

Isaiah dumped the camera and the two undeveloped pictures into his bag, then followed Allison as she moved away from the basement. James, meanwhile, continued to rub his head in the spot where he'd hit the cuckoo clock. For something so cute, it sure could pack a punch.

It wasn't long before the house was packed with people, and all the earlier drama had been forgotten. The Biddle house was proving to be the perfect venue for a Halloween party.

"Hey, Margot!" Lucas called out, sidling up beside her. "I dig your costume. What are you, like, a sexy Keanu Reeves?" he asked, eyeing her conservative trench coat.

"I'm a spy," Margot deadpanned, sliding sunglasses over her face.

Lucas grinned. "A spy would never say that."

Margot studied Lucas's face, which was covered in even more cuts, bruises, and stitches than usual—half drawn on, half real. "I see you came as yourself."

"No," Lucas said with a goofy laugh. "I came as a 'guy with brain damage.'" Then he held up a red cup and wiggled it in front of Margot's face. "Check out what I found in the kitchen."

Margot peered into the cup. It was full of wriggling worms. Lucas reached in and pulled one out, dangling it over his open mouth. "They're worms. I'm not sure what kind, but I'll probably google it. Wanna see me eat one?"

"So glad I came," Margot grumbled, feeling—once again—like she did at school pep rallies. She would never, ever fit in with this crowd. She glanced across the room just in time to catch the end of Allison and Isaiah's heated conversation.

"I wouldn't have cared that you invited her, but you made it weird," Allison was saying to him.

"It's not a big deal," Isaiah protested. "She helped me with something, so I invited her."

Allison put her hands on her hips. "Helped you with what? What can she help you with that I can't? I'm your *girlfriend*. Why are you always talking to her?"

"We've been neighbors forever," Isaiah reminded her. "Babe, I talk to the postman, too. Are you jealous of the postman?"

"If the postman was a girl your age who you were always talking to, yes." Allison rolled her eyes. Then she looked over and noticed Margot watching them. "I can't do this anymore." She groaned, then stormed off.

Margot wandered over to Isaiah. "I'm going to head out."

"Why?" Isaiah tried to play it cool, but he knew she'd over-heard Allison's accusations.

"You know why," Margot said, echoing his own thoughts aloud. "Why didn't you tell Allison I was coming?"

"I don't know. It just seemed easier to avoid it." Isaiah sighed. "Look, things have been weird. Allison's just stressed."

"No," Margot said, shaking her head. "Don't make this all about Allison. I actually like Allison. And now she hates me, because of some crap you pulled. I don't appreciate you pitting us against each other."

"I'm not pitting anyone against anyone!" Isaiah said, defensive. "How am I pitting?"

"You can only talk to me when your girlfriend's not around," Margot scoffed. She did not want to be *that* girl—the one who got in the way of someone else's relationship. "I'm not the girl you cheat with. Not on tests and not at parties." She turned and walked away, leaving Isaiah standing alone.

Suddenly, the lights in the Biddle house began to flicker. At first, Isaiah wondered if the same thing was happening that had happened before the party started, but then he spun around and spotted a middle-aged dude standing at the entrance to the house.

"Hey, everyone," said Nathan, flicking the light switch off and on again. "We're officially closed for the evening. So sorry for ruining your Halloween, teens who are enthusiastically trashing my new house. Now take off before I call the cops."

"There's an old creeper here!" someone yelled from deep within the party. "Everyone out!" The crowd scattered. Outside, Lucas and Isaiah split off from the pack. Others ran for the road. Many dove for cover in the trees.

Allison, meanwhile, headed into the woods—alone. Almost as soon as she got past the first few trees, she realized she never should have left Isaiah. Here she was, outside the haunted Biddle house, by herself. On Halloween, no less.

She slowed to a walk, her breathing heavy, when she realized she'd totally lost her way. Which way was back? Where was the road? She began to panic, realizing that she could be stuck out here all night—or longer. But then, *yes*, just up ahead was some other kid. "Hey," she called out as a greeting. "You took off, too?"

The kid said nothing. Whoever it was just spun around to face her, his face hidden by shadows. There was something about him that felt off—creepy, almost. The way he stared at her was unsettling. Messed up.

"Um . . ." Allison said, taking a timid step backward. She tried talking to him again, hoping maybe he just hadn't heard her question the first time. "Do you know the way back to the road?"

The kid just stared back, silent and still. He said nothing.

Allison spun and tracked back through the forest the way she'd come. Any direction was better than going toward that weirdo. She'd try to backtrack instead. She would see headlights or the glow from the Biddle house eventually. But a few moments later, the same kid was standing straight ahead of her, blocking the path. She drew up short, her breath ragged. *What the—?*

"How did—" she began, her eyes wide. Before she could finish her sentence, the kid began to come straight at her, at full speed. Allison screamed, turned, and ran.

Her heart thudded in her chest. Branches scraped at her face and arms, ripped at her outfit, and tangled in her hair as she tore through the woods. But Allison didn't care about any of that. All she cared about was getting away from whoever was out here in the woods with her.

But just moments later, she crashed into a solid body as she reached the crest of a hill. It was him—again.

He was after her. And now he'd found her.

As Allison tried desperately to distance herself, the figure was reaching, his face twisted with anger and something else—something horrific—as he grabbed for her, his hands catching, twisting, and grabbing.

Allison tried one more time to get away, but she jerked too far. She screamed in terror as she plummeted down the hill behind her, flailing her arms to try to stop her fall. Just before she hit the ground at the bottom, crumpling into a twisted heap, she got a clear view of her assailant's face. And what she saw made her wonder if she hadn't survived the fall.

For there, at the top of the hill, was some kid screaming back at her, his face melting off his skull before his head burst into flames.

CHAPTER EIGHT

"Allison will be okay," Isaiah told James the next day at school. Allison had been pretty shaken up after the party, but she wouldn't talk about what had happened in the woods after the homeowner had busted their party. Isaiah shrugged it off as her usual drama. "She seemed spooked, but she's saying it was just a bad prank."

"I'm glad she's all right," James said.

"Where were you the whole time? You missed all the excitement."

"Sam and I generated plenty of excitement on our own." James smirked. "I'm waiting for you to ask me." He paused, then went on without Isaiah asking anything. "We made out. Kind of. It was brief."

Isaiah stopped his friend's story short as he noticed a familiar face at the cafeteria doors. "Oh, crap," he said. "That's the dude who broke up the party. Don't look. He doesn't know who we are."

"I'm looking for Isaiah Howard?" Nathan called out over the din of the cafeteria.

James raised his hand and pointed at his best friend. "He's right here." Then he scrambled up, tossing out a hasty, "Sorry, Isaiah, I have anxiety."

Nathan strolled over and tossed Isaiah's backpack on the table. "I believe you left this at my house last night."

"Oh, that *is* my bag," Isaiah said, grinning innocently. "It was kind of you to drive it all the way over here."

Nathan nodded. "I was coming here, anyway. I'm your new English teacher, Mr. Bratt."

Isaiah blanched. "Oh, uh, I have no idea how that ended up at your house, sir. Also, I love English. I speak it all the time."

Mr. Bratt waved him off. "I was your age once. I know how fun it is to make terrible decisions. So I'm not even that mad about it. Let's pretend it never happened. No one's parents need to find out." Isaiah stared back at him, incredulous. Was this guy for real?

Mr. Bratt went on, "In return, you will spread the word among the usual suspects that, moving forward, my house is a place where a human now lives and is therefore no longer a party destination."

As Mr. Bratt strolled away, Isaiah let out a deep sigh of relief. Then he dug in his backpack to see what he'd accidentally left at the old Biddle house the night before. Inside his bag were two now-developed Polaroid pictures—the only problem was, they weren't the pictures Isaiah had taken. In fact, he had no idea what he was seeing. In the first, Allison was screaming—her mouth and eyes wide open in terror—as she fell backward down a hill in the forest. In the second, Margot was choking and grabbing at her throat as she laid on the ground next to a vending machine at school.

Isaiah stared at the horrible pictures, his mouth hanging open. "What the hell?"

Later that afternoon, Margot stopped by the vending machine in the main hall at school to grab a snack. She carefully punched in the number for her usual nut-free bar and waited as it dispensed. The halls were empty, but suddenly Margot noticed movement at the far end of the hallway.

A kid stood there, frozen, his face hidden in shadows. He was staring straight at her, his whole vibe giving her the creeps. "Can I help you?" she called out. The dude didn't reply. Margot took a bite of her bar, giving him another look. Just as the bell rang to signal the end of class, the kid took off and the halls filled—right as Margot realized she couldn't breathe.

"Are you okay?" Isabella said, running toward her.

Isaiah ran in behind her and fell to the ground next to his friend. "Nut allergy! Get the nurse." He bent down to rip open Margot's bag. "Tell me you have your EpiPen." As soon as he pulled out the EpiPen, he slammed it into her leg—and Margot's throat cleared enough for her to catch a small, shallow breath.

"I'm okay," Margot coughed out, just as the nurse and Margot's dad appeared on scene to help. As the school nurse and Mr. Stokes led Margot away, Isaiah backed up and pulled the Polaroid picture out of his backpack. Somehow, the photo of Margot depicted the exact scene he'd just witnessed.

"You have to see these," Isaiah said, running to find James after school that day. He pulled the bizarre photos out of his bag, flashing them in front of his friend's face.

"See what?" James asked.

Isaiah spun the pictures around. They were blank. Just undeveloped Polaroid sheets. But he knew what he'd seen. He would never forget the tortured faces of his girlfriend or his oldest friend that he'd seen in the photographs earlier that day. They had looked terrified, both of them in grave danger. And now the photos were just . . . blank? There's no way he had imagined something that messed up. "No," he said, waving the blank photos in the air. "These were the pictures of Allison and Margot. The ones I took in the house, but before what actually happened to them. Which is impossible—"

"Okay, okay, slow down. I don't understand anything you're saying." James gave him a wary look, one that told him he wasn't really buying Isaiah's story.

"This camera is haunted!" Isaiah screamed. "It's a haunted camera. You have to believe me, James."

James studied his friend, who was *not* acting like himself. He softened when he realized why Isaiah was freaking out. "You think it's haunted because you found it in the basement where that kid died."

"Yes! Exactly."

"Makes perfect sense," James said. "Can I see the camera, please?"

"Be careful," Isaiah said, gingerly handing the old camera to his best friend. "There's, like, cursed devil stuff going on there."

James turned the camera in his hands, inspecting it from every angle. Then he lifted it and snapped a picture of Isaiah. The flash erupted. James grinned. "Say cheese."

"Whoa, no!" Isaiah said, grabbing the camera back. "Why would you do that?"

"Because the camera is not cursed or haunted," James said, rolling his eyes. "There is no such thing as an evil Polaroid camera. That isn't real." He hopped in his Jeep and drove away, leaving Isaiah alone in the rain to watch as the picture his friend had just snapped came into focus.

It was a shot of Isaiah, all right. But it wasn't the picture his best friend had just taken. Instead, the photo showed Isaiah laying on the football field, his arm badly broken, during tomorrow night's big game.

Isaiah was completely freaked out. What was going on with the camera he'd found in the basement of the Biddle house? He'd been trying to figure it out—and trying to understand what he had to do to break whatever kind of curse he'd unlocked—but he was at a loss. He looked out his front window and saw Margot heading home from school. He ran outside to greet her. "Hey, Margot."

Margot smiled at him. "Hey, I was going to come see you. Thanks for, you know, saving my life. I still can't believe I picked the wrong bar from the vending machine. I've never made that mistake before." She suddenly noticed how fidgety and nervous Isaiah seemed. "Is something wrong?"

"Yes, actually. Take a look at this." He pulled out the Polaroid picture of himself, badly injured on the football field, but as soon as he flashed it in front of his friend's face, the image disappeared. He shook the camera in the air and growled, "You won't let me show anyone, will you?"

"Why are you talking to that camera?" Margot asked.

"Because it's trying to ruin my future."

"What?"

"It's why you had an allergic reaction," Isaiah explained.

"No, I had an allergic reaction because I ate the wrong bar."

"No, it's just like what happened to Allison. And if I play in tomorrow night's game, I'm its next victim. But if I *don't* play, the scouts will skip me over. Either way, it's got me trapped." He leaned in toward Margot, his face pleading. "I really need your help, Margot."

"I don't believe this." Margot shook her head. This was typical Isaiah. "I thought you were actually checking up on me. To see how I was doing for a change. But you made it all about *you*—again. I don't know what's going on with you right now, but I can't be the person you only talk to when you're having problems."

"Please, Margot," Isaiah begged. She was the only one he could trust with this. Even his best friend had ignored his concerns. "Just hear me out. I swear this time is different."

Margot spun on a heel and walked away. She was sick of Isaiah only paying attention to her when he needed something. What about the *rest* of the time? "I'm sorry, Isaiah. You're going to have to solve this problem on your own."

Isaiah glared down at the camera. Margot was right about one thing—he had to solve this problem. Before the game. Before that picture told a *real* story. "You can't hurt me if you don't exist," he growled at the camera. Running inside the house, he set the camera on a table in his garage. Then he grabbed a mallet hanging on the wall and raised it over his head. He swung down, smashing the camera over and over again until it was a crumpled pile of parts scattered across the tabletop.

Then he poured lighter fluid over the mess of pieces and set them on fire. "I'm going to play that game," he said with a snarl. "I'm going to *win* that game. And there's nothing you can do about it!" Then he tossed the blank picture into the fire, too, watching as it melted away.

CHAPTER NINE

Everyone showed up for the big game. This was it—Isaiah's chance to show all those scouts he was worthy of a scholarship. He was worthy of a future. He was *someone*.

The crowd seemed to sense their quarterback's excitement, and everyone was cheering wildly in the stands. It didn't hurt that the Titans were already up by six in the first half, all thanks to Isaiah. And the fans weren't the only ones excited. The scouts were taking notice, too.

Inside the locker room at halftime, Isaiah pumped up his teammates. "What did I tell you? What did I *tell* you? This is our year! This is our time!"

Coach Rifkin clapped him on the back and reminded the team, "Okay, we still have another half. Let's get out there. Keep up the intensity and finish strong!"

The other players roared as they grabbed their helmets out of their lockers and ran back out to the field. But as Isaiah reached in to grab his helmet, he stopped short. Right there on the shelf in front of him was the Polaroid camera. The very one he'd broken into bits, burned, and destroyed. It was back and in perfect condition, and it was waiting for him.

Isaiah exited the locker room in a trance. What did this mean? How was this *possible*?

As he ran onto the field, Isaiah was terrified about what might happen. What if the picture James had taken of him came true, the way the pictures of Allison and Margot had? He spun around, motioning to his coach that he needed a sub. He had to figure this out before that picture became real. There was more than the game on the line. His *life* was on the line.

"You just went in!" Coach Rifkin called back, waving him off.

Someone grabbed Isaiah by the jersey and tugged him into the huddle. "What's the play?" his center asked.

"Uh, okay, look—right now it's not about plays. It's about goals. What's our goal here?"

"To . . . win?" someone guessed.

"No," Isaiah said. "It's to protect the QB. That is our goal. Even if it means we lose." The team lined up for their first play of the second half. Isaiah's breathing went ragged as his mind kept flashing back to that picture. Him, unconscious and badly injured on this field, tonight.

"Call the snap, Isaiah," his center barked at him.

Isaiah couldn't do it. He had to get off the field, no matter what the cost. He spun around to the ref, calling for a time-out. The ref looked back at him—but it wasn't the ref they'd had during the first half. Now it was some kid—someone his age—he didn't recognize, glaring at him from inside the ref's uniform. Isaiah's eyes went wide as the kid's head began to melt and then erupted into flames, his face morphing into a grotesque mask of terror.

For a long moment, Isaiah stood frozen, trapped in his own

fear. No one else on the team or in the stands seemed to notice what Isaiah was seeing—except one person. Lucas's mom, Nora, seemed to sense something was very wrong from the stands. Could she see the burning kid, too, or was Isaiah living in this nightmare alone?

With a look of dread, Nora leaped to her feet as Isaiah began to weave through the field, avoiding seemingly invisible foes. He wasn't playing the football game anymore—he seemed to be playing some other sort of game. One that had him terrified. "Stop the game!" Nora screamed as she watched Isaiah run toward the end zone. "Please, someone stop the game!"

To Isaiah's eyes, the opposing team had all turned into fiery monsters, and the ball was melting in his hands. He was being pursued, chased down, and attacked by a swarm of flaming beasts and no one other than him could see it happening.

Isaiah put everything he had into running toward the end zone. He was almost there. If only he could end the play, maybe he could get off the field and make this horror stop. But just as he was about to cross over the line for a touchdown, a pair of hands shot out of the field, like a zombie at a graveyard. Spindly fingers wrapped around Isaiah's ankles, pulling him down, tripping him up. It was too much for him to shake off. With one last, beastly scream, Isaiah thudded to the ground, writhing in pain as dirt-crusted hands dragged him down.

Isaiah immediately knew his arm was broken. He looked down and could see the bone sticking out of his skin at an odd angle. He was bloody, broken . . . and an exact re-creation of the photograph that had come out of Harold's Polaroid camera that afternoon. Isaiah screamed again, and then the world went black.

"How you doin', champ?" Isaiah's dad asked when he woke up in the hospital later that night.

"Did we win?" Isaiah asked.

"Yes," Ben said. "Not that it matters. I just talked to the doctor, and based on your age and the X-rays, she feels optimistic. If you get after your physical therapy, you should make a full recovery."

"How long?"

Ben took a deep breath. "If things go smoothly, six to eight months."

"That'll knock me out for the rest of the season," Isaiah said, watching his future disappear just like the image on the Polaroid had when he tried to show it to Margot. "I'll miss my scholarship window!"

"You just focus on healing," Ben told him, sharing a look with Laura, Isaiah's mom. "Now get some sleep." He slipped out of his son's hospital room. Just outside the door, he found Nora pacing back and forth in the hospital hallway. "Nora, what are you doing here?"

Nora looked at him, her face filled with panic. "It doesn't end with Isaiah. He's going to visit the sins of the parents on all the children."

"What are you talking about?" Ben asked, stepping back.

Nora put her hand on Ben's arm. "He's come back, Ben. Harold Biddle. He's come back to make us pay for what we did to him."

CHAPTER TEN

L ife had returned to the old Biddle house. Settled in front of the fireplace, Nathan realized he was starting to love this place. Curses and tragedy be damned. He would turn this tortured old house into a cozy home with a happy future.

Suddenly, the fire in the fireplace snuffed out. Nathan set down his crossword puzzle and stepped toward the hearth to investigate. He flicked a match, tossing it into the fireplace, but it wouldn't catch, even though there was plenty of wood left to kindle. Looking across the living room, Nathan noticed that the old basement door was *open*. That was weird. He still had the stitches he'd gotten while trying, and failing, to pry it open a few days earlier.

"Guys, c'mon," he called out, figuring it was probably teenagers again, trying to find *somewhere* to party. Well, that somewhere wasn't *his* house, that was for sure. "I thought we had a deal. This is no longer a party destination." He spun around, ready to defend his turf against stupid teens.

But instead, what he saw on the other side of his living room froze Nathan into place.

For there, standing across his living room, was Harold Biddle. As Nathan locked eyes with him, the long-dead teen began to levitate, and in the next instant, he burst into flames. Just as Nathan began to scream, the charred, angry remains of Harold streamed directly into Nathan's open mouth.

PART TWO

— *Isabella* —

THE HAUNTED
MASK

CHAPTER ELEVEN

Isabella was used to being invisible.

She'd learned to navigate the halls of Port Lawrence High School as a shadow, seeing but never seen. In fact, she'd used her invisibility to create a superpower: hidden Internet troll, calling out every jerk who deserved being taken down a notch.

On Halloween morning, Isabella served herself and her little brother cereal, just as she did every day. Plus an extra dash of cinnamon for Alan, because he was amazing, and he deserved it. There was nothing she wouldn't do for her kid brother. Afterward, she put on her uniform of invisibility—a just-cute-enough sweater and skirt, her camera bag, and a neutral, bored expression hidden behind loose, straight brown hair—and made her way through the halls of PLHS, wondering if maybe today would be different; maybe today would be the day someone noticed her.

Isabella entered the weight room, where the football team was just finishing up morning practice. "Look, Isaiah," Coach was saying. "Friday there's gonna be a college scout in the stands—I had to convince him to take a look at you, so this is the night you have to deliver. Dig deep and push hard. It can't be just a good game; it's gotta be your best game ever."

Isaiah was focusing on what Coach Rifkin was saying, but Isabella could sense his nerves as the star quarterback took in his coach's words. This scout thing was freaking Isaiah out. That was one of the benefits of being invisible—you learn to read people, see things no one else notices.

"Hey, Coach," Isabella said, once he'd finished up with Isaiah. "I have that footage you asked for." She held up a tape including the last football game she'd filmed from the sidelines. Never sitting with the student section, Isabella was always lurking around the edges, watching as life played out around her.

Coach brushed past her without a word or a glance. He didn't even notice her there. She slipped the footage back in her bag and left.

Upstairs at her locker, Isabella listened quietly as Margot and her dad, the school's guidance counselor, had a tense conversation just outside Mr. Stokes's office. "So, Mom's not coming back from Seattle this weekend?" Margot asked her dad.

"I'm sure she feels terrible," Mr. Stokes said, not sounding entirely convinced. "Maybe she has a big photo shoot this week."

"Why doesn't she want to spend her birthday with her daughter and her husband, like a normal mom?"

Mr. Stokes sighed. "You would have to ask her, honey."

"Yeah," Margot said, brushing past her dad. "Like she's going to tell me anything."

As Margot rushed by, Isabella reached out a hand. "Are you okay?"

But Margot didn't hear her; she just continued down the hallway.

As Isabella headed up the stairs toward her first class of the day, she jumped out of the way when someone came flying down the stairs on a skateboard. "Lucas!" Isabella screamed, reaching

down to pick up her phone, which she'd dropped in the near colli-
sion. "You almost killed me!"

"Sorry," Lucas said, shrugging. "I didn't see you."

Isabella growled under her breath. She buried her face in her
phone, retreating from this god-awful high school to hide out
online—the one place where she knew she could get people to
notice her. As she passed students in the halls, she anonymously
posted comments to each of her classmates' social media profiles:

Daddy pay for the lips, or just the nose?

Nice shirt, does it come in your size?

You suck so hard you blow.

Can't believe they let you out of the womb!

Ever see someone so ugly your eyes sting?

Isabella grinned. This was power. This was how she could
make an impact.

She was so caught up in her phone that she didn't notice
Allison, who was walking right toward her. Isabella slammed into
the popular girlfriend of the star quarterback and fumbled her phone
for a moment.

"Excuse you, clumsy," Allison snapped.

"Sorry, Allison!" Isabella called back. "I was distracted,
and . . ." But Allison had already moved on and found her people,
leaving Isabella forgotten once more.

"What time is the party?" Allison's friend Wendy asked as the
two girls headed down the hall. Isabella had heard about this party,
but as usual, she wasn't on the guest list.

"Eight," Allison said, grinning.

"What time is it ending?" Wendy asked.

"Sunrise? 'Cause that's when my parents get home from upstate!"

The two of them laughed. Isabella sat with this information for a second. Suddenly, she had an idea. She pulled up Allison's parents' Insta accounts and put her plan in motion. If she wasn't invited, no one should be. What good was a troll if it wasn't powerful enough to do some damage?

CHAPTER TWELVE

"Look what I found," Alan said, prancing into Isabella's room later that day. "Your old vampiress costume."

Isabella shook her head. "Why would I go to a party I tried to sabotage?" Somehow, Allison's friends had come through for her and found a new venue for the party that night. Isabella's plan had failed—and now the It Girl's party was on again, despite Isabella's efforts to ruin it.

"You tried and failed," Alan pointed out. "I say it's fate. Come on, don't you want to see the Biddle death house in person?"

"Not my thing. Anyway, I was twelve when I last wore this thing."

"So?" Alan asked with a shrug. "Vampires never go out of style. They literally can't. Cause they live forever . . . cause they're vampires."

"Please stop explaining your joke."

"Whatever. You should go, 'cause you're anxious and miserable and a party might make you happy."

Isabella flopped onto her bed. "I can't."

"Why?"

"Because nobody knows me at school. I'm literally invisible to them."

"Maybe that's 'cause you never join in. What's the worst that could happen?"

As soon as she arrived at the party, Isabella knew she'd made a mistake. Everywhere she turned, she could sense people staring at her, judging her, wondering why *she* had come.

Why *had* she come?

Ducking through an open doorway, Isabella found herself alone. She took a deep breath, trying to muster up the courage to reenter the party. But then, she heard someone whispering her name. *"Isabella . . ."*

She spun around, searching for the source of the voice.

A door in the corner of the room swung open with a creak, and Isabella stepped forward, curious. *"Isabella . . ."* Slowly, cautiously, she followed the voice down the stairs to the basement. *The* basement. The very place where Harold Biddle had died in that awful fire, all those years ago. At the bottom of the stairs, she explored the space using only the scraps of light slicing in from the slim windows at the top of the basement walls.

Suddenly, she noticed a plaster mask sitting atop the worktable on one end of the basement. She reached forward, and the voice urged her on. *"You deserve to be seen . . ."* it whispered. *"Just put me on."* Isabella placed the mask over her face and felt a jolt of electricity course through her. She straightened up, then studied her reflection.

She stepped toward the bottom step, ready to reenter the party in her new disguise. It was worth a shot, if only to see how it felt to play someone else for a while.

Upstairs, behind her mask, Isabella felt freer than she ever had. She stepped out of the shadows for once, moving through the party like a person who mattered, a person who was worth noticing, a person worth everyone's time.

It was the greatest she'd ever felt, and she wasn't going to let that feeling—or her new mask—go. Not now that she knew just how amazing it felt to be someone else for a change.

CHAPTER THIRTEEN

Later that weekend, Margot swung by Isaiah's house to see how his arm was feeling. "Hey," she said, slipping in through the side door. "I'm not bothering you, am I?"

"Nah," Isaiah answered. "I'm good." Truth be told, he was *not* good. He couldn't reach James to tell him what he'd seen at the game on Friday night, that he had a badly broken arm, and all the other weird stuff that was happening. So no, *not* good. He reached for a baking tray of brownies, to clear off a chair for his friend to sit, but knocked his cast against the table instead. He winced—doing stuff with one arm was not fun.

"Isaiah!" Margot said, reaching for the brownies. She hated seeing him in pain. "Let me do that."

"I got it."

"You have a broken arm."

"Thanks, Margot," he snapped back. "I hadn't noticed."

Margot cringed. "That was me expressing empathy, badly."

"You're not bad at it. Everything just sucks right now. Here, sit." She sat, scanning the heaping piles of brownies and cookies and breads that loaded the table. Isaiah explained, "Every five minutes, someone shows up with a new baked good."

"So what happens now?" Margot asked, gesturing to his arm.

"Rehab. They're saying six months, minimum." Isaiah sighed.

It still hadn't totally hit him—that he was out. Done for the season. Maybe forever. "I mean, that's after I get the cast off, which could be a month or two. So scholarship's up in the air. Everything's kind of . . . up in the air."

"I'm sorry about the other day." Margot frowned. "You were in trouble and I threw it all back in your face."

Isaiah stood up—he didn't want to talk about this with her. "Yeah, well . . . Hey, you want any of this mess? One of these must not have peanuts, I'm sure."

"Isaiah," she said, reaching out to touch his arm. "The stuff you told me about the camera . . ."

Ignoring her, he continued to rifle through the plates and platters of treats. "Okay, all of these contain nuts. Literally any of these could kill you. Why put nuts into baked goods? It's like putting avocado on a BLT. Way to ruin a perfectly good thing—"

"Isaiah!" She quickly stood up, trying to catch his attention. "I *saw* you on the field. Something was clearly wrong." He studied her, wondering what it had looked like from the stands. Had anyone seen what he'd seen that night? That kid in flames coming after him? Margot asked, "What exactly did you see out there before you broke your arm?"

Isaiah considered telling her, but then he shook his head. "You're better off staying far away from this."

"Far away from what?"

"Thanks for stopping by," he said, waiting for Margot to leave so he could figure out what he was supposed to do with his life now.

CHAPTER FOURTEEN

O n Monday morning, Nathan woke up on the floor of his living
room. "Ow," he moaned, rubbing his head and his stiff limbs
after a rough night. "Ow, owww." It was the first time he'd been
alert since his visit from Harold earlier that weekend. "Monday?"
Nathan gasped, staring at his watch in disbelief. How on earth was
it *Monday*? He'd slept through the entire weekend. He rushed toward
his front door—he had school. Kids were waiting for him. His new
job was waiting for him.

But as Nathan ran toward his front door, his legs betrayed him
and he fell over in a heap. His arms wriggled as if they had a brain
of their own and were operating separately from the rest of his body.
Nathan stood up and shook himself off, then climbed into his car
and sped toward school.

As he ran through the halls of PLHS just before the first bell,
Nathan's body continued to revolt. With each step, it was as though
his mind wanted to do one thing, but his body chose to do another.
He flopped like a fish, his legs jerking and writhing in two different
directions. Rushing into the bathroom, Nathan splashed water on
his face. He had to get it together.

"What is wrong with me?" he asked, lifting his head to look in
the mirror. What he found looking back at him provided no comfort:
the reflection he saw in the bathroom mirror was Harold Biddle.

"Augh!" Nathan screamed, looking over his shoulder. There was no one else in the bathroom with him. He glanced in the mirror again, his eyes locking with Harold's. "You're not real . . . ?"

Harold glared back at Nathan, then he hissed, "Help me . . . find him."

Nathan yelled back, "Leave me alone!" Suddenly, Nathan's body convulsed. As he locked eyes with Harold in the bathroom mirror, his body shook—and Harold's spirit fully entered and completely took over Nathan's body.

Bye-bye, Nathan Bratt.

Welcome back, Harold Biddle.

CHAPTER FIFTEEN

"Hey, Susan," Isaiah called out to Isabella as she operated her drone camera at football practice later that afternoon. She was there every day, but this was the first time anyone had ever really noticed her presence. Isabella patted her bag, making sure the mask was still there, right where she'd tucked it before leaving for school that morning. Something about it gave her comfort and confidence. She felt more whole when it was beside her.

"Hey," Isabella called back.

"You shoot footage of all the games, right?" he asked.

"I do."

"Can you get me Friday's?" Isaiah wandered over to her, glancing at the remote control in her hands.

"You mean," Isabella began, "when . . . ?" Isaiah nodded. Yep, he needed to see the play where he broke his arm. "You sure you want to see that?"

He shrugged. "You watch film to learn from your mistakes and get better, right? Why should this game be any different?"

"It's on my AV cart," Isabella said, nodding toward the school. She glanced at the other video coordinator, hoping she could trust him with the drone. She landed it gently. "Can you watch the drone for me?"

The other guy shrugged. "Sure."

Isabella grabbed her backpack, then she and Isaiah headed inside so she could pull up the footage. "How long have you done AV club?" Isaiah asked as Isabella searched through her film.

"Since freshman year."

"You know what's weird?" he asked. "We've been in school together for years, and I know, like, nothing about you."

"Including my name," she said, glancing up at him briefly. "It's not Susan. It's Isabella."

"For real?"

"Yeah."

"I'm sorry," Isaiah said, and she could tell he meant it. "I didn't . . ."

"It's okay." She shrugged, then paused the film—she'd found the play he was looking for. "Do you want me to hang around?"

"Nah, I got it from here, Susan." He grinned. "Thanks."

"No problem, Isaac," she said, grinning back at him.

Heading back toward the practice field, Isabella heard the distinctive sound of her drone—flying. "What the hell?" She raced toward the field just in time to see Lucas at the top of the bleachers, her drone floating in midair just above him. "Lucas!" she screamed.

Lucas leaped off the top of the bleachers, grabbing on to the two drone rails with each of his hands. It was obvious he thought the drone had enough power to support his weight and keep him airborne; it did not. The drone spiraled wildly, then dropped to the ground along with its passenger—both of them crashing onto the asphalt below.

By some miracle, Lucas escaped from his stunt with just a few cuts and bruises. Isabella's drone, however, suffered a much worse fate. "I'm really sorry, Mr. Stokes," Lucas said, sitting beside Isabella in the guidance counselor's office. "I swear I will never hang from a stolen drone again."

Mr. Stokes nodded. "Don't apologize to me, Lucas. It's not my drone."

Lucas glanced at Isabella, who was heartbroken. The drone had cost a fortune. She'd protected it as carefully as she would a living pet. And this idiot had just single-handedly destroyed it?

Lucas aimed puppy-dog eyes at her and said, "Look, in my defense, I didn't know it was yours." He shrugged. "I thought I was destroying *school* property, which is a totally different thing. And I honestly thought drones were way more durable. Like, you hear people talk about when the robots take over and kill off humanity, and so you figure that it wouldn't be so easy to beat up a robot."

Listening to Lucas's "apology," Isabella grew more and more annoyed. This wasn't an apology—it was an excuse! She glanced down and saw the mask looking up at her from inside her bag. Suddenly, she could hear it whisper to her: *You know he doesn't mean it. He's a liar.*

"Lucas," Mr. Stokes said, cutting Lucas off. "I think you need to do more than apologize. You need to make good on this financially."

Lucas nodded. "Oh, okay. Well, how about, I'll give you five bucks a week until the drone is paid for?"

"Okay . . ." Mr. Stokes said, glancing at Isabella. "That's *an* offer. Does that seem like something both parties can agree to?"

"Yeah," Isabella murmured.

But from inside her bag, the mask disagreed. *"No . . . do not back down."*

Isabella suddenly snapped. "No, you know what? No. That drone cost three thousand dollars. And if this moron somehow manages to graduate, he will never make that money back flipping burgers the rest of his life."

"Whoa," Lucas said, clearly caught off guard. "Why is this chick so intense?"

Mr. Stokes held up his hands to calm her down. "I don't think she meant that. Tempers are just running hot—"

"Oh," Isabella said, her smile as fake as Lucas's apology. "Oh, no. This 'chick' did mean all that. I'm just telling Lucas to his face what everyone says behind his back. You are a pathetic person. This whole *Jackass* facade—"

"Whoa," Mr. Stokes broke in. "Can we dial it down a bit?"

Isabella sneered at him. "How's this? You're a high school guidance counselor. You literally failed at life."

"I care about helping kids," Mr. Stokes argued.

Isabella shook her head and stood up, leaning toward him over the desk. "Here's the thing, *Colin*. You didn't help me. So now my mom is going to kill me. *Kill* me. And it's because you're an idiot."

She pointed at Lucas, then turned her attention back to Mr. Stokes. "And *you're* worse than an idiot. You're weak." She paused, glancing down into her bag again. The mask had gone still, and suddenly, *she* felt like the idiot. "Sorry," she said hastily, grabbing her bag and racing toward the door. "I'm sorry—don't worry about the money. Five bucks a week is fine."

As soon as she was gone, Lucas opened his mouth. "So . . . is that settled, then?"

"Yeah," Colin said with a sigh. "Just go to detention now."

CHAPTER SIXTEEN

O nce Isaiah had finished watching Isabella's tape from the game, he headed for the locker room. He already missed it—the smells, the team, the hope. He couldn't believe he wouldn't be in this locker room, leading his team to victory for the rest of the season. He opened his locker. It was time to take care of that Polaroid camera, the one that seemed to be the source of so many problems.

But when he opened his locker, it was empty. The camera was gone. Suddenly, a loud whistle screeched behind him and Isaiah spun around, rattled. There was Mr. Bratt, the new English teacher, standing behind him in a ref uniform.

"Sorry!" Mr. Bratt said with a grin. "Didn't mean to scare you. I'm training to be a new ref. Whistle works."

"It sure does," Isaiah said, nodding.

"You know," Mr. Bratt said, stepping closer to Isaiah. "Your dad, he did some work on my house. He used to play football here, too, right?"

"He did," Isaiah answered slowly. "How did you know that?"

"I know a lot about my students."

Isaiah gave him a weird look. Something about Mr. Bratt made him seriously uncomfortable. "Well . . ." he said, sidestepping past his new teacher to get to the door. "I should get going."

Bratt nodded at him. "Sorry about the arm."

"Not your fault," Isaiah said with a shrug.

Mr. Bratt grinned again, then began to laugh.

Isaiah hightailed it out of there. That hadn't been a joke; why was the dude laughing?

Later that afternoon, Nathan stopped into the Harbor Stop just as Nora was closing up for the night. "Sorry," she called out to him as the bells jangled on the door. "We're not open for dinner."

"Oh noooo," Nathan said, pouting like a child. "I was really in the mood for an egg sandwich."

"Um, okay," Nora said after it was clear he wasn't going to turn around and leave. "Sure, I can heat one up."

"Thanks. I'm new in town and have been wanting to try this spot."

"Oh, wait," Nora said, grabbing an egg sandwich out of the case. "Are you Mr. Bratt?"

Nathan didn't reply for a second, then suddenly jumped a bit as if he'd just realized the question was intended for him. "Yes! Yes, I am Nathan Bratt. The new English teacher."

"My son loves you," Nora told him, popping the sandwich into the microwave. "Well, he said you're 'not the worst,' which is really the highest compliment you can get from him these days." Ever since Lucas's dad had died, Nora had been having trouble connecting with her son. He just seemed so reckless and disconnected—it had been nice to hear him saying something positive for a change. "Do you live close to here?"

"No," Nathan said. "I'm actually on the edge of town. The old Biddle house."

"The Biddle house?" Nora said, spinning around with her eyebrows raised. "How long have you lived there?"

"Just a few days."

Nora grabbed the sandwich out of the microwave and began to package it up. "You know, everyone thinks it's haunted. Do you? I mean, have you noticed anything strange going on?"

Nathan considered this. "No. Not that I can think of. I did hear the horrible story of the boy who lived there, though."

"Harold," Nora said, nodding. "Yes, it was sad."

"Kids can be so cruel."

"What do you mean?" Nora asked. She couldn't help but wonder how much Nathan knew about the night Harold had died. Did he know what she knew?

"Just that, it seems like everyone forgot about him and moved on."

Nora took a deep breath. "Not everyone." She reached down to grab a bag for his sandwich, and when she stood up, Nathan was nowhere to be found. She glanced around—where did he go? Suddenly, she turned, and there he was, standing just inches from her, back behind the counter. "You can't be back here," she said, breathless.

Nathan smiled and reached over her head. "I just wanted to grab one of these. Cocoa." He ripped open the packet and dumped the contents straight into his mouth. Then he turned to go, calling out, "Thanks, Nora," over his shoulder.

Nora watched him walk away, wondering, *How does he know my name?*

CHAPTER SEVENTEEN

Later that night, Nora caught up with Isaiah as he was taking a bag of trash out to the curb. "Here," she said, holding open the bin so he could toss the bag up and in with his good hand. "Let me help."

"Thanks." Isaiah nodded toward the house. "My dad's inside."

"I came to talk to you, actually." Nora reached into her bag, but her hand froze when Ben, Isaiah's dad and one of Nora's oldest friends, stepped out of the house.

"Go inside, Isaiah," Ben called out. "I'll be there in a minute."

Isaiah gave the two adults a confused look, then stepped back inside, leaving his dad and Nora alone in the dark. "I told you," Ben said with a hiss. "I don't want your dark, woo-woo crap around my family. He's been through enough."

"Ben," Nora pleaded. If anyone could understand what was happening, it was him. "Just hear me out—"

"About what? Harold? His ghost broke my son's arm?" Ben frowned. "Is that what you're saying?"

Nora groaned. "I don't know exactly *what* I'm saying."

"Go home, Nora. This is getting sad."

He returned to the house. Just as Nora was about to head home herself, she spotted Margot coming down the sidewalk. "Hey, Margot," she called, hustling toward the girl.

"Um, hey, Ms. Parker."

"Do me a favor?" Nora asked, reaching into her bag. "Give this to Isaiah. Ask him if he recognizes this kid." Then she scurried off without another word.

"Where did you get this?" Isaiah asked, holding the photograph at arm's length.

Margot could tell he recognized the kid in the picture, but from where? It was an old picture, and it definitely wasn't someone they knew from school. "From Nora. Do you know him?"

"Yeah, I do," Isaiah said. He couldn't believe he was about to say this, but he didn't have much of a choice. "I saw him on the football field. He was the referee that night . . . Then he was on fire. Who is he?"

"I did some research," Margot said. "I'm pretty sure it's Harold Biddle."

"What?" Isaiah said, his eyes snapping up to meet hers. "The kid that died in that house?"

"We have to talk to Nora," Margot said. "She obviously knows something she's not telling us."

CHAPTER EIGHTEEN

"Izzy, check this out," Isabella's little brother, Alan, held out his phone so she could see what he was watching. Ever since idiot Lucas had broken her drone, she'd been grounded—from all her devices, the Internet, her *life*. Which meant she hadn't been online at all. The truth was, it wasn't her drone at all. It was her *dad's* drone, and it had been broken on her watch. When she hadn't even gotten permission to take it from him in the first place. So now she had to pay for Lucas's stupidity when she shouldn't have even been *caught* borrowing the drone in the first place.

"I'm not in the mood, dude," she said, not wanting to watch one of Alan's little kid videos as her first entry back into her online world.

"Just look," Alan said, holding the phone closer. "It's evidence."

She leaned in. It was video footage of Lucas's stunt—someone had captured the whole thing on video. "Are you kidding me?" Isabella said. "He *posted* this?"

"We can show this to Dad," Alan told her. "Show him it wasn't your fault."

"No, I'll handle this."

"What are we going to do?" Alan asked, bouncing.

"*We're* not doing anything. I'm handling it." She shoved her brother out of her room and slammed the door. As soon as she was alone, she could hear the mask calling to her: *"Let me help you . . ."*

Isabella took a deep breath. She threw on a black hoodie and black jeans, and grabbed the mask off her bed. It was go time. She put the mask over her face, and she sucked in a sharp, sudden breath when it immediately fused to her skin, becoming one with her. She was ready to show the world what happens when you mess with Isabella one too many times.

Outside the Harbor Stop, Lucas was working on his skateboarding moves—again. Anything to get out of his own head. Tricks were the only place he could find peace anymore; they gave him an escape, a chance to focus on *physical* pain instead of the crap going on in his own head.

"Hello?" Lucas called as he heard someone across the parking lot. A dark, hooded figure emerged from the shadows, dragging one of his skateboards. "Yo! Don't drag the board! It's expensive."

Suddenly, the figure lifted the skateboard overhead and flung it straight at Lucas. It sailed through the air at top speed, knocking him off his board. Lucas cowered on the ground as the hooded figure stormed toward him. He held his skateboard up as a shield. "Hey, chill!"

But the board was no match for the figure's fury. The hooded figure slammed fisted hands into Lucas's skateboard and broke it in two. Grabbing the pieces, the attacker then slammed them into

Lucas, nailing him in the back so hard that he sailed through the air into a pile of crab traps. He was immediately knocked unconscious.

The figure slinked toward his lifeless body, finally pushing back her hood as she stood over his helpless form.

Fueled by rage and power, the mask on Isabella's face began to transform, morphing into a monstrous troll. Her ears stretched and twisted; her hands became gnarled claws. Standing over Lucas's body, Isabella the troll lifted the jagged skateboard over her head once more—ready to finish the job.

But before she could bring the board down, an oar smashed into Isabella from behind, knocking her to the side. "Get away from him!" Isaiah cried, rushing toward the troll with the same intensity he'd had during his final play of Friday's game.

"Back off!" Margot screamed, stepping up to stand beside Isaiah.

The troll roared at both of them before slipping away into the darkness.

Isaiah looked at Margot, his eyes wild. "What the hell was that?!"

CHAPTER NINETEEN

Late that night, Alan had just fallen asleep when he heard sounds coming from somewhere in the kitchen below. With his mom at work and dad out of town, he knew it must be Isabella—finally home from wherever she'd disappeared to.

But the noises were loud and scary—and wrong. He could hear something crashing in the dining room, and then something broke. Creeping toward the sound, Alan got a look at the kitchen and saw the whole place had been ransacked. Things were strewn everywhere.

That's when Alan realized the sounds were not being made by his sister, but some kind of intruder. He made his way toward the house phone, stepping gingerly so as not to attract attention. His big sister would know what to do. But just as he reached for the phone, he got a glimpse of the . . . *thing* in the kitchen. It was a *troll*, ugly and wretched and very, very angry.

He picked up the receiver and hastily called Isabella's number. *Please pick up*, he begged silently. But after a second, his sister's ringtone sounded—from inside the troll's pocket! "Izzy?" he whispered, staring at the awful beast that was in possession of his sister's phone. Did it hurt her?! But then suddenly he had another, more horrifying realization: Could this troll . . . *be* Izzy somehow?

The troll turned on him, roaring as Alan screamed. He tossed the phone at the monster, running for the backyard. Alan raced to the old playhouse, figuring it was the best place to hide. From his perch up in the trees, Alan could see the troll emerge from the back door. It sniffed, searching for any sign of him.

Alan sat as still and quiet as possible, watching, terrified, as the troll's shadow sniffed and searched around the yard. The playhouse had slits that let in just enough light for Alan to catch every shadow, to wonder at every movement on the other side of the wall where he was hidden. Suddenly, the troll stepped inside the playhouse. Alan choked back a scream, watching as the troll's pointy ears twitched, listening—for him.

The troll turned, and moonlight hit its face. For the first time, Alan could get a good look at it—and it was far more horrible than he'd originally thought. Alan continued to stay frozen, hoping its senses weren't able to pick up his breath and scent. As soon as the troll exited through the front door of the playhouse, Alan released his shaking breath.

And then, the troll's arm came bursting through the wooden slats at the front of the structure—searching, reaching, grabbing for him. "Izzy!" Alan screamed. "Stop!"

The troll sprang back into the playhouse and scrabbled for the squirming kid. "This isn't you!" Alan sobbed.

Now his sister loomed over him, his fear fueling her monstrosity. The energy coursing through her veins was power. Complete and total power. She wasn't invisible now.

"Please!" Alan tried again. This was his sister. Somewhere below that horrible, monstrous facade was his sister—his kind, loving sister. His person. The one who took care of him and comforted him when he was scared. And now she was the one doing the scaring. "Stop this! Isabella!" Now he was in tears. His breathing hitched with a distinctive whistling sound—the sound he made when he was at his most frightened. "I'm here. It's Alan. It's me!"

Suddenly, something seemed to connect with the troll. Recognition—love for her brother—snapped Isabella out of the mask's control. Gazing down at herself through the mask, Isabella noticed her hands had turned into claws. "No," she cried, stepping back. "Get off me!" She scrabbled at the mask, trying to pry it off her face. But the mask was determined to hold on and maintain power over her, to give her the strength it knew she needed to finally be noticed.

Then, with one final rip, she managed to pry the mask off her face and hurl it to the playhouse floor. Her hands morphed back from claws to fingers, her ears retreating, her body standing upright again. She gasped, body still adjusting to the sudden transformation, as she spun around to check on her brother. "It's okay," she cooed as she moved toward him. "It's me. I promise it's me. I'm so sorry," she repeated over and over. Alan looked unsure until finally Isabella reached forward and pulled him into a hug. An Izzy hug. His sister was back.

The next morning, Isabella and her brother stood at the rail of a small bridge near their house. Isabella cradled the mask in her hands, holding it carefully, understanding the power it could have if she allowed it. "I have no idea what just happened," she told her brother. "But I'm glad it's over."

"Yeah," Alan said softly.

"I'm really sorry I hurt you, Alan. I hurt a lot of people."

"It's okay," Alan said bumping against her. "It wasn't you, not really."

"But it was a little. That's the part I'm sorry for." Isabella held the mask up, studying it again. "Do you think Mom will ever forgive me for destroying the kitchen?"

"Oh no," Alan said, cringing. "You're going to be grounded for, like, a year."

"Still better than trying to convince her an evil mask made me do it."

Alan laughed. Just as the mask began to speak to Isabella again, she dropped it into the water below. "Should we say a prayer or something?" Alan asked as the mask bubbled to the bottom of the water.

"Rot in hell?" Isabella suggested.

"Rot in hell," Alan agreed.

As soon as they'd walked away, leaving the mask at the bottom of the stream, a figure emerged from behind a nearby tree. Quickly, with purpose, Nathan raced toward the edge of the bridge. Then he reached down and plucked the mask out of the water.

CHAPTER TWENTY

The next day, Isabella rode along with her mom to visit one of her old high school friends—James's mom, Eliza. "I don't know why I had to come and Alan got to stay home alone."

"Because at the moment, I don't know if I can trust you," Victoria told her daughter as she parked the car in front of the massive house.

"I said I was sorry." Isabella felt like all she'd done was apologize since the night the mask had possessed her. She knew that's what she had to do, but she wished her mom would just accept the apology already.

"I hope you mean it," Victoria said. She led Isabella onto Eliza's wide, elegant front porch.

Eliza swung open the door and looked surprised. "You brought Isabella."

"I'm sorry, Eliza," Victoria said. "It's been a rough couple of days."

Eliza called out to her son over her shoulder. "James! Take Isabella to the game room, please."

"Hi, Iz," James said, waving for her to follow him. "Come on."

Outside in Eliza's backyard, the old high school friend group gathered: Isaiah's dad, Ben; Lucas's mom, Nora; James's mom, Eliza; and Isabella's mom, Victoria.

"How do we get you to stop with this ghost nonsense?" Ben asked Nora, once they were all seated across from one another.

"I'm telling you guys," Nora said. "He's back. And I think he's coming for our children."

Ben groaned. "Listen to yourself, Nora. That's the kind of talk that will get you in trouble again."

"I wasn't crazy then, and I'm not crazy now," Nora told them. They had to believe her. There were just too many coincidences to be anything *other* than Harold Biddle.

"You could lose custody of Lucas," Victoria cautioned her.

"Are you guys threatening me?" Nora asked, standing up.

"I think the threat," Eliza added, "is really to Lucas, who could spend his last years in high school without a mom."

Nora glared at her. "You're one to talk. At least I'm present in my son's life rather than drowning myself in wine." Then she stormed out, frustrated and betrayed by her so-called friends.

Inside the game room, James and Isabella killed time playing billiards. Isabella watched as Nora stormed off, but she couldn't hear exactly what was being said.

"What are they fighting about?" James asked.

"It sounds like your mom is really laying into Nora," Isabella said, watching as James lined up his cue stick.

"She does that on her second bottle," James deadpanned. Isabella laughed, but James did not. It was way too close to the truth. He gestured to Isabella. "Your shot."

Isabella lined up her shot. She and James both leaned over the table, across from each other. Isabella took a couple small practice shots, then drew back her cue stick and fired. Her stick hit the ball hard, too close to the table, and it sailed up into the air—straight at James.

The moment the ball struck his forehead, James exploded— and a nasty shower of goop splattered across Isabella and the billiard table. Suddenly alone in the room with nothing more than her pool cue and a puddle of goo that had just moments ago been her classmate, Isabella opened her mouth and screamed.

PART THREE

— *James* —

THE CUCKOO CLOCK OF DOOM

CHAPTER TWENTY-ONE

For James, the worst part about their epic Halloween party at the Biddle house—yeah, the one that ended with a crabby teacher busting things up—had been getting hit in the head with that stupid cuckoo clock.

The *best* part about their epic Halloween party, though, had definitely been James's make-out sesh with Sam. Things had been building between the two of them for so long, and that night, James had felt *hot* in his costume. Sexy Cat, Sexy James. But their first ever real convo hadn't gone at all how James had planned. Luckily, it was the *last* conversation that counted.

Things started when James bumped into Sam in a corner of the party and muttered, "'Sup."

"'Sup," Sam had replied.

"I'm James. From your Spanish class. *Hola*." He hoped Sam already knew who he was, but just in case—he didn't want to make it awkward.

"Oh, yeah. I know."

"So," James said, taking in Sam's athletic costume. He gave him a flirty smile. "Aerobics instructor. Super campy. I love the costume."

Sam glanced down. "Oh, thanks. A lot of this stuff I really work out in. I just added a wristband."

"Oh." James didn't know how to take this. The dude was fit, but—well, this was a surprise. A hot surprise. "Cool. Yeah, I love to work out, too."

"Oh, yeah?"

"Yeah." James grinned.

"You play a sport?" Sam asked.

"Not, like, right now. But I have."

"What sport?"

"Soccer," James spat out before he had time to consider the options.

"I love soccer. You follow any teams?"

"Uh," James said, faltering. "London United."

"It's . . . Manchester United."

James laughed. "Yeah, I just mean the British one. Go, London!"

"There's, like, seven teams in London," Sam said, his forehead creased. "And none of them are called 'London.'"

"That's confusing," James said, feeling embarrassed.

"I have to go," Sam had said, backing away.

"Wait," James called after him. "Where are you going?"

As soon as Sam took off, James found Isaiah. "How'd it go?" Isaiah asked.

"Brutal. He was very, very not at all interested in me."

"Were you being yourself?" Isaiah asked. James was amazing—sometimes, though, he didn't recognize his best gifts and tried to be the person he thought someone else wanted him to be instead.

"Of course," James lied. "So . . . he may have asked me if I was into sports, and I may have said yes, even though I may not be at all."

"You gotta be yourself, man. You can't be so obsessed with being liked."

James flopped back against the couch. "I'm just trying to be friendly."

"What if you don't try so hard? Just be James."

James side-eyed him. "Well, that's an easy thing for you to say."

"What does that mean?" Isaiah asked.

James rolled his eyes. Whatever. He wasn't going to bring the mood down. "Nothing, man. It's all good. I think I'm gonna bounce. Happy Halloween."

James sidled through the crowd, rubbing his head where he had knocked into the cuckoo clock earlier. It was starting to throb, and the music sounded almost fuzzy. He had to get out of there and get some sleep.

But as soon as James walked out of the house and stepped off the front porch, his body jolted and the pain in his head intensified to brain-cracking levels. He blinked, stepped backward, and a second later was opening his eyes and sitting up on the floor below the cuckoo clock again.

"Ow," he moaned, rubbing his head. Now it *really* hurt.

Cuckoo, cuckoo, cuckoo!

James stirred and began to stand up, listening to his friends chattering around him—and froze when he realized he'd already heard this whole conversation play out before.

Margot looked down at him with a worried look on her face. "You okay, James?"

"Where did everyone go?" James asked. "The party was happening, and now it's . . . before?"

Isaiah studied him. "Do you wanna sit this one out, or do you want—"

"—to go show everybody how a Sexy Cat gets down?" James repeated the end of his best friend's sentence along with Isaiah—since he'd already heard the line before. Earlier that same night. A few hours ago, when they'd first had this exact conversation. James scrambled to his feet and ran for the door.

But again, as soon as he stepped off the front porch, he was launched back to *before* the party, after he'd been hit in the head.

Cuckoo, cuckoo, cuckoo!

Again, James listened to his friends go through the *exact same conversation*. "I think I'm in a time loop," he muttered.

"Please, no bits," Isaiah snapped. "We have to set up a whole party, and there's no time for James jokes."

"No, I literally just came from the future," James tried to explain.

Isaiah laughed. "Okay, then, let's get rich. Who wins the Super Bowl?"

James ran for the door again, but then he stopped and decided to try another exit. Just like before, as soon as he stepped away from the house, he flipped back in time and woke up below that awful clock.

Cuckoo, cuckoo, cuckoo!

Over and over again, James tried every possible exit in the

house. But no matter what he tried—even jumping off the roof—he couldn't seem to leave. He just landed back in the same spot again and again, right below the cuckoo clock.

Cuckoo, cuckoo, cuckoo!

He was seemingly stuck in the Biddle house.

After so many failed attempts, James just couldn't try again. He let the party play out—but he wasn't his usual bubbly self. Instead, he sat in a heap at the bottom of the stairs, glaring at the cuckoo clock, knowing it was somehow the source of his torment.

"Excuse me," someone said from a few stairs up, "can you just . . ." James slid over to let Sam through, then went back to sulking. It was completely out of character. "You okay?" Sam asked, sensing the disconnect from the usually chipper James and this puddle of misery on the stairs.

"I'm trapped in a nightmare," James answered honestly. "And it won't stop. It just keeps repeating, over and over. Every time I try to escape it, I wind up right back where I started."

He slumped, and Sam plunked down beside him. "Sounds like you're in high school. Sometimes all you can do is make the best out of a bad situation." Sam smiled at him, and James brightened. If he was stuck in this stupid time loop, at least he could play it to his advantage. Make the best of a bad thing and all.

"Hey," James called out as Sam headed back into the heart of the party. "What's your favorite soccer team?"

"What?" Sam asked, intrigued. "Why?"

"Just tell me."

"Arsenal," Sam said with a shrug.

The next time that scene played out again, James was ready. He'd done a few hasty Google searches, then stepped off the porch to rewind to the beginning of the night again.

When Sam asked him to slide over so he could pass James on the stairs, James played the same sad-boy part again.

"You okay?" Sam asked, right on cue.

"I'm just so bummed about Arsenal." James sighed. "My favorite soccer team. They haven't been the same since Vieira left."

Sam grinned at him. "I love Arsenal, too. And I totally agree! His ego—"

"—basically destroyed the team," James continued for him, nodding. "But at least they have Øegaard, right?"

The two guys smiled at each other, totally vibing.

And *that's* what led to the make-out sesh. Soccer, of all things. Oh, and a messed-up cuckoo clock.

After they'd been making out for a while, Sam pulled away and looked James in the eye. "You wanna get out of here?"

James smirked. "More than you know."

As they headed for the door, they passed the cuckoo clock again. James grabbed Sam's arm and said, "I'll be right with you." Then he turned back, walked up to the clockface, and stopped the minute hand from ticking. Finally, he opened the little bird door and glared at the critter inside. "Bite me."

As James walked out the front door, he glanced down at Sam, waiting for him in the yard, just beyond the porch. Beyond that magic threshold. He paused. Would it work this time? Did he figure out how to get past the curse?

"What's wrong?" Sam asked, noticing James's hesitation.

"Just trying to stay in the moment," James said, taking a deep breath . . . then he stepped off the porch and walked toward his guy. "Let's get out of here."

CHAPTER TWENTY-TWO

The next morning, James woke up in the best mood of his life. His headache was gone, he'd had an *amazing* night with Sam, and he'd missed the whole party-getting-busted part of the night for something *much* better.

As he grabbed a package of Pop-Tarts from the cupboard, James felt his phone vibrate with an incoming text: *Morning, Sexy Cat. We should watch a Real Madrid game together sometime.*

James hummed and began singing his thoughts to himself. "What is Real Madrid? I don't know anything about soccer . . . don't really care. But Sam is hot."

He opened the fridge and grabbed the milk from inside the door. He twisted off the cap, then took a swig straight out of the carton. It wasn't as if his mom would notice—the woman only drank wine, anyway. He slammed the door closed, and let out a shrill screech.

For there, on the other side of the fridge door, was . . . himself. Dressed in his Sexy Cat costume from the party the night before.

"Not very sanitary," the other James scolded him.

"What the—" James shrieked.

"Hell is happening?" another Cat James asked, strutting into the room.

A third copy of James sauntered down the stairs and explained, "Every time you went through the time loop—"

A fourth James went on, "You created a duplicate version of yourself."

"That's not how time travel works!" James protested.

"It's not how a cuckoo clock works, either," said another James as he weaved across the kitchen.

James backed away from all the copies of himself and ran out the front door. "Isaiah," he said, patting his pockets. "Isaiah will help me." He stopped, patting his pockets again.

The gaggle of James duplicates paraded through the front door, one of them holding James's phone and keys in his hand. "Looking for this?"

"Don't worry," said another dupe. "You won't be late for class."

Another sneered at him and added, "You won't have to worry about being late ever again."

Then the two closest duplicates tossed a burlap bag over James's head and threw him into horrible, terrifying darkness.

The duplicates carted him to James's family's old, abandoned copper mine, where they dumped him onto the wooden floor and snatched the burlap sack off his head. James scanned his surroundings. On one side, a row of windows; on another . . . a pit. A deep, endless pit with a chute that led down into even more blackness.

"Help! HELP!" James screamed.

"No one's coming to help you," the first duplicate told him, still smirking beneath James's own costume ears.

"Why are you doing this?" James begged. "Because of that clock?"

"There's a whole lot more to this than just a clock, James."

"Whatever this is, it won't work. People will know you're not me," James told them. That had to be true, right? Everyone could see through a fake?

"No, they won't," one duplicate said.

"They won't even know you're missing," said the other. "They don't even know who you really are."

With that, the duplicates tossed James off the wooden walkway, and he plummeted down the mine shaft. As he fell into the abyss, the sound of James's voice slowly faded until he could no longer be heard at all.

CHAPTER
TWENTY-THREE

The next morning, a *new* James showed up at school. This duplicate was ready to make a fresh debut. It was time to stir some things up.

"Hey, Allison," Dupe James said, hitting up his friend at her locker. "Did you see where Isaiah and Margot went off to?"

"No," Allison said, frowning, her eyebrows raising in alarm. "Why, what are they doing?"

"Everything," Dupe James said. "They are inseparable. Like, if I didn't know you guys were a thing, I'd be all 'What is going on with those two?' Anyway, see ya!"

Meanwhile, another Dupe James set some new boundaries with Sam.

"You asked me to meet you," Sam snapped. "And then you didn't show. I waited for an hour."

"You're so clingy," Dupe James said, rolling his eyes. As if he hadn't been busy doing more important things. "I thought jocks were supposed to be standoffish and cool. You're always whining at me!"

"I'm not whining!" Sam said. "I'm asking for some consideration."

Dupe James sighed. This guy was too much.

"You know what?" Sam said, looking disappointed. "I'm done."

"No," Dupe James said. "*I'm* done."

Then he took off. It was *fun* messing with someone else's life.

The next day, across town, a different Dupe James racked up a game of pool with Isabella while Eliza and Victoria were having their weird old person meeting with their high school friends. When the pool ball hit his head and he exploded into a mess of goo, Isabella screamed. She had no idea this James was fake. Who could even tell what was fake and what was real, anyway?

"What happened?" Victoria cried, running into the room just in time to see Isabella standing at the pool table, covered in a coat of green goo. Ben and Eliza flanked her on either side.

"It's . . . it's *James!*" she shrieked. "He exploded." Turning to the spot where James had been standing just a moment earlier, she now found . . . James. He was back?

"I *what?*" the replacement Dupe James said, smirking at her.

"What's going on?" Isabella asked, wiping the goo out of her eyes. She knew what she'd seen, but now that James was standing there, maybe she . . . No. She'd seen it happen. "Don't look at me like that," she told the small crowd of parents. "James exploded. See the slime?"

Dupe James laughed. "Practical joke gone wrong. The ol' sack of slime gag has always been hit or miss."

"That's not true," Isabella said, pointing a finger at him.

"Izzy and I will clean it up," James told the parents. He moved toward her.

"You stay away from me," Isabella screamed, backing away from him while holding up a pool cue as a weapon.

"Isabella!" Victoria yelled, grabbing her daughter's arm. "What has gotten into you?"

"I don't know who that is," Isabella said, pointing at Dupe James. "But it's not James."

"Sweetie, give me the pool cue," Ben said gently.

As Victoria rushed Isabella out the door, she called back, "Eliza, I am so sorry."

Eliza sighed, then turned to Dupe James. He cleared the nasty grin off his face just in time to keep her from seeing it. "Clean up your mess."

Ben guided Eliza toward the front hallway. "What the hell was that?"

"It's kids being kids," Eliza said, chuckling. "Don't let Nora get under your skin." Ben nodded, but all of a sudden, he wasn't convinced. Too many weird coincidences lately, and this whole scene felt . . . off. Eliza sighed. "You want any more wine? I might open another bottle."

Ben shook his head. "No thanks. It *is* a weekday."

As he left, Eliza rolled her eyes and mimicked him mocking her. "'It *is* a weekday.'"

She poured another glass.

CHAPTER TWENTY-FOUR

"That *was* a monster at the Harbor Stop, Isaiah," Margot said later that day. She and Isaiah were hanging out at his house, trying to figure out what exactly had been going on when they rescued Lucas.

"Is that possible?" Isaiah asked.

"That's what we saw," Margot reminded him. "Whatever broke his skateboard wasn't human."

"It doesn't make any sense."

Margot looked at him seriously. "Isaiah, you saw a ghost on the football field. You had a camera that predicted horrible things happening to people. None of this makes sense!"

"So, what do we do?"

"I don't know!" Margot cried, throwing her hands up in the air.

"I'm not asking you to know," Isaiah reminded her. "I was just asking." He dropped his good arm over her shoulder, trying to comfort her. "You don't have to fix this alone."

Margot glanced at him, briefly wondering if maybe that spark she felt between them was mutual. They had always been old friends, nothing more. But maybe . . . Just then, Isaiah's dad, Ben, came into the house.

"Hey, Dad," Isaiah said, quickly scooting away from Margot and removing his arm from her shoulder.

"Hey, Mr. Howard. How's it going?"

"It's going." Ben sighed.

Margot and Isaiah shared a look: *What's up with him?*

"We need to talk to James," Margot said. Maybe he could help figure this out.

Margot and Isaiah caught up with James before lunch at school the next day.

"James, where are you going?" Margot called out as a duplicate of their friend headed for the parking lot.

"We've been looking for you," Isaiah called out.

Dupe James scoffed. "I'm skipping. Is there a problem, officer?"

"Yes," Isaiah said. "And you haven't been answering any of my texts. C'mon, man, I thought you were dead."

"We need to talk," Margot pressed, chasing after him. "There's some weird stuff going on."

"You don't need to tell me. I already know," Dupe James said, grinning. He gestured to the two of them, making a lewd gesture. "You two, getting freaky behind Allison's back. It's all good, I approve."

"No, no," Isaiah protested, even though he knew how this whole situation might look—to some people. "That's not what's happening."

"That's not what Allison thinks," Dupe James teased.

"Guys, we have more important things to be talking about here," Margot broke in.

"This about that dumb camera again?" Dupe James asked, finally spinning around.

"We fought a monster," Margot said, knowing it was going to land weird. It *was* weird. But it was the truth.

Dupe James looked at her like she was crazy. "Margot, stop. Seriously, I expect this from Isaiah but not from you."

"Why are you being like this?" Isaiah glared at him.

"Why?" Dupe James sneered. "You blew it at the big game, Isaiah. Not because of a *magic camera*, but because you're just not that good at football." Before he could clock his best friend's reaction, he spun to Margot and added, "And you. Pretending to believe in ghosts will not make Isaiah like you. This whole crush thing was cute when we were seven. Grow up."

"Apologize to her right now," Isaiah demanded.

"Or what?" Dupe James laughed. "You gonna hit me?"

Splat! A baseball bat came swinging down on James's head and he instantly exploded into a spray of goop.

Both Isaiah and Margot screamed.

James was gone. Behind where he'd been standing, Isabella stood poised with a wooden bat in her hands. She leveled them both with a look and said, "We need to talk. Some weird stuff has been happening."

"You just blew up James," Margot blurted.

"I didn't," Isabella said.

"But you did," Isaiah pointed out, shaking goop off his fingers.

"I really didn't," Isabella promised. "Can we please talk?"

"Okay," Isaiah said. "But does anyone else smell watermelon Jolly Ranchers?"

Margot sniffed at the goop on her hands. "Oh my god, you're totally right."

"Honestly, it's the weirdest thing about all this," Isabella said, shaking her own limbs to get the slime off.

Isaiah jumped away, trying to avoid getting any stray dupe goop. "Stop! I don't want James juice on me!"

Inside the AV room, Isabella filled Margot and Isaiah in on what had happened to her with the mask.

"You're the monster we saw?" Isaiah gasped.

"It wasn't me!" Isabella said. "I mean, the troll was me, but it was really the mask. And now something's happening to James."

"He's splattering," Margot noted.

"That wasn't James," Isabella reminded them. "That was, like, a copy or something."

"So . . . where's *our* James?" Isaiah asked.

Isabella shrugged. "Missing. Or worse."

"We can figure this out," Isaiah said, trying to keep his cool. "James needs us to."

"Isabella, where did you get the mask?" Margot asked.

"The Biddle house on Halloween night," Isabella told her.

"That's where I found the camera," Isaiah said.

Margot's eyes went wide. "Oh my god, it's connected. It's all connected."

Isaiah nodded slowly. "So maybe what's happening to James started there, too."

"We need to know more about Biddle," Isabella said.

"I know exactly who to ask."

"This isn't a good time, guys," Nora said, glancing up to find Margot, Isaiah, and Isabella holding up her photo of Harold Biddle. She could still hear Ben's voice in her mind, warning her to stop with the crazy. Stop acting like this was something more than it was.

"Why did you ask me to show Isaiah this photo?" Margot asked her, sliding it across the counter.

"That was a mistake." Nora sighed and looked at Isaiah. "Your father is right. I should mind my own business."

"Wait," Isaiah said. "My dad told you not to talk to me. Why?"

"Just tell us what's going on," Isabella said as Nora grew more and more uncomfortable. "You obviously know."

"I can't talk about this with you," Nora said seriously.

"I've seen him," Isaiah said, pointing down at the picture of Harold. "You've seen him, too, haven't you?"

Nora fidgeted but stayed silent.

"Nora," Margot tried one more time. "James is in real trouble, and it's because of that house and this kid."

Nora finally leaned in, her voice low. She looked directly at Margot and said, "If you want answers, *ask your mother.*"

CHAPTER TWENTY-FIVE

Back at the Biddle house, things were really rocking. Nathan had fully undergone his transformation to Harold Biddle and was now reminiscing by reliving some of Harold's fondest activities from high school in the months before he'd died.

Biddle-Bratt gently returned his beloved mask to its stand, carefully crafted a few new scrapbook pages, and then made a snack. Pouring hot chocolate powder and milk into a cereal bowl, he then dug in . . . to a big bowl of wriggling worms and chocolate milk.

With a crunch, Biddle-Bratt chewed and grinned, enjoying a combination of his favorite snack from then—hot chocolate powder—and his favorite snack *now*—tasty worms.

Suddenly, the music he'd been listening to on Harold's old CD player began to skip. "Oh, you gotta be friggin' kidding me!" he screamed. Biddle-Bratt stormed into the living room and began to pound at the CD player with a broom. His rage was obviously simmering just below the surface and ready to boil over at any moment. Just as he was really getting into his destruction act, the doorbell rang. His head flew up. He wasn't expecting company; no one ever stopped by. He peeked out the door and saw Colin Stokes, the school guidance counselor.

"Coming!" Biddle-Bratt said, calming himself before opening the door.

"Hey," Colin said, peeking past him. "Is everything okay? I just heard a racket."

Bratt looked confused. "Really? I didn't hear anything."

"Okay . . ." Colin said. He'd been sure he'd heard pounding, but maybe not.

"Wanna come in?" Bratt said, his face bright and hopeful.

"If I'm not overstepping," Colin said.

"Of course not!" Bratt said, swinging his door open wide. "Come on in!"

"Look," Colin said, settling into a chair across from Bratt. The teacher was slurping out of a chocolate milk box, which Colin found oddly unsettling. But hey, everyone had their thing, right? "I just wanted to come by because I heard about the kids crashing your house on Halloween. It's sort of my responsibility to follow up on these things, since everyone at the party probably goes to PLHS." Colin folded his hands together. "If you want to pursue disciplinary action, there are official channels . . ."

"Oh," Bratt said, laughing loudly. "If I wanted to discipline these kids, I don't think I'd go through 'official channels.'"

Colin smiled at what he assumed was a joke. "Well, I suppose we can file this party matter under, 'kids will be kids.' My wife, Sarah, and I used to go pretty hard back in the day."

Bratt's head snapped up when he heard that name. "Sarah? Is Sarah from Port Lawrence?"

"Oh, yeah." Colin laughed. "PLHS girl. Go, Titans!" Bratt grew suddenly serious and alert. This was a name he knew, a name that mattered more to him than any of the others. Luckily, Colin didn't seem to notice his change in expression. He continued talking, "But that was all before life happened and things got complicated."

"So things are," Bratt said, studying him carefully, "rocky between you two?"

"We're living apart right now," Colin explained. "It's complicated."

"Okay," Bratt said, then took another long, slurping sip of his chocolate milk.

Colin quirked his head. He couldn't quite get a read on Nathan. "Anyway," he said, standing up to brush off his slacks. "I better let you get back to it."

"This was fun!" Bratt said, trailing after Colin toward the door. "We should do it again."

"Definitely," Colin said, sounding less certain than the word implied.

"Thanks for the company!" Bratt said, waving as Colin hustled off the front porch.

CHAPTER TWENTY-SIX

James was sick of waiting. Waiting for someone to rescue him, waiting for someone to tell him what was going to happen next, waiting for whatever cruel fate was around the corner. He was tired of someone else calling the shots, always. So he began to search through the rubble at the bottom of the mine shaft, looking for anything he might be able to use to help him escape.

Just as he was about to give up his search and collapse, James felt something hard beneath his fingertips. He pulled out an old miner's bag and flipped it open. There, inside the bag, was a pickax and hammer. He spun around, studying the fallen beams that had broken under the weight of his body when he'd fallen to the bottom of the pit.

A ladder. If he could build a high enough ladder, he could slip out into the night and make a run for it. He began to build, using the tools he'd found.

After hours of work, James knew he was close. He began to climb, dragging his tools along with him. He took one step, another, then another. Each step was more timid than the last. He didn't want his makeshift, rotting wood ladder to collapse. The wood creaked under his weight, and he could hear the squeak of nails as the contraption began to give. "You can do this," he said aloud, hoping it was true. "You're the Sexy Cat. Sexy Cat can climb anything."

Just as he could see over the edge of the pit, James took another step, and his foot broke through the ladder. He went careening down, slamming against a platform halfway down that helped to break his fall before he hit the bottom again.

He was right back where he started, but now he was even more bruised and broken than before. He was going to die in here; it might be time to accept it.

Meanwhile, James's friends were pursuing every lead they could think of to find him. "While we wait, we *could* do what Nora said," Isabella suggested as she, Margot, and Isaiah kept watch over James's house. "We could ask Margot's mom."

"Let's not. She's pretty busy right now," Margot said, shooting Isabella down.

"Oh, yeah?" Isaiah asked.

"She's doing her professional photography thing. She's getting into some really weird artsy stuff," Margot explained. Then she cut herself off, pointing at the just-opened front door of James's house. Some version of James had just come outside.

Isabella immediately pulled out a hammer, ready to bash another body into goo. But Isaiah pulled her arm back, reminding her, "We're here to follow him. We don't learn anything if we pop him."

"Besides," Margot added. "It is possible that's the real James."

Disappointed, Isabella put away her hammer. She followed, hopping in the car. The threesome trailed behind James as he drove through town, then made his way to a more rural area and pulled the Jeep to the side of the road.

"Why is he going to his family's old mine?" Isabella asked.

"Let's go," Isaiah said, hopping out of the car to follow James up a dirt road.

They followed their friend—or a duplicate version of their friend—as he headed inside the abandoned copper mine. James walked ahead of them, his flashlight bobbing like a beacon for them to follow from a distance.

Water dripped from the cold stone walls, and puddles splashed under their feet. Still, they carefully followed James, trying to figure out where he could be headed.

Suddenly, a light flashed right in their eyes. "Oh, hey!" called out a voice that *sounded* like James, but couldn't actually be their real friend. "Looks like this is a trap?" An old mine car began to roll in their direction, gaining speed as it came careening toward them. The three friends turned and ran the opposite way.

But they were stopped short by *more* James duplicates. "Dead end," one of them droned. They were boxed in, trapped by duplicates on every side.

Just then, a panicked voice called out from a different direction. "Over here! It's me. The real me!" It was James—again. The real, or another fake? Either way, he offered an alternative to the situation they currently found themselves in. James waved them over urgently. "I figured out the tunnels, c'mon!"

They had no choice but to follow him. It was better than sitting in the middle of a trap. Isaiah, Margot, and Isabella hustled after him, finally stopping when they reached a big room inside the mine.

"James, what is going on?" Isaiah asked, now that they had some space and time to talk.

James explained, "It was the clock. I repeated the party, and it repeated me . . . somehow. I don't know!"

Then, another James called out from somewhere nearby. "Watch out! He's leading you into a trap!"

"No, I'm not," said James.

"Yes, he is," argued the other James. "If you go that way, he's going to drop you into a pit. That's what they did to me. *I'm* the real James!"

"No, I'm the real James."

"No, I'm the real James. Of course the dupe's going to try to impersonate me. It's so first thought."

"No, calling your own bit 'first thought' is what's first thought, you hack. *I'm* James, Isaiah! We're like brothers!"

Isaiah was completely confused. He had no idea who was real, who was fake, who to trust. He looked at both dupes, who both smiled at him in the same way. Then, without a second thought, Isaiah grabbed a board and clocked one of the James's over the head with a board and he exploded into goop.

A second later, the other James grinned and said, "Actually, none of us are the real James." Another duplicate appeared, and then another. Margot and Isabella took off running, but Isaiah was caught by a pair of dupes. They threw a burlap sack over his head and tossed him into a pit.

"That guy was the worst," one Dupe James said.

The other Dupe James nodded. "Tell me about it."

Below, Isaiah rolled to a stop at the bottom of the mine shaft. "Isaiah!" the real James cheered, his voice hoarse. "You came for me! I knew you would find me. I've been down here for so long. I thought I was going to die!"

Isaiah scrambled to his feet, grabbed a rock, and knocked James over the head.

"WHAT IN THE HELL?" James screamed at him.

"Sorry," Isaiah said when James didn't explode into goop. "I didn't know if you were a dupe or really you."

"How could you not know it was really me?" James asked, hurt. "I'm your best friend. You're supposed to know if it's me or not."

Isaiah nodded. "Okay, I can see that it's been hard for you down here. But just chill, and let's try to find a way out—"

"Is this why it took you so long to look for me?" James asked. "Because you can't tell the difference between your best friend and one of those monsters?"

"They were *impersonating* you," Isaiah reminded him. "And I kinda had my own stuff to deal with." He *still* hadn't had a chance to fill James in on everything that had happened at the game on Friday. Dude had been MIA since the Halloween party—now he finally understood why.

"You know what I was dealing with?" James snapped. "Drinking dirt water and starving to death while my best friend doesn't even know who I am."

"Look, dude. Those dupes are good at impersonating you. I'll just leave it at that."

"What does that mean?" James put his hands on his hips.

"You're not always yourself, James. You change who you are based on who you're with. So, it wasn't as easy as it sounds to tell who the real James was."

James snorted. "It's a lot easier for you to be yourself. You're the star quarterback! You've been popular since first grade. It's harder to be one of six gay people in an entire town."

Before Isaiah could respond, rocks tumbled along the wall, and a sledgehammer crashed through an opening in the rocks. Isabella and Margot leaned in.

"How did you find us?" Isaiah asked them.

"We were able to follow your voices," Isabella told him. "Because you were talking about your feelings for so long."

"Hurry," Margot said, motioning for the guys to follow. "We know the way out!"

Isaiah and James climbed up the rocks and scrambled through the opening that Margot and Isabella had bashed open for them. Together, the four friends ran for the exit. Margot and Isabella made it through, but before Isaiah and James could slip past the door to freedom, it slammed shut.

Once again, they were surrounded by fakes.

James and Isaiah were trapped inside a cave within the mine, swarmed on all sides by James duplicates. Violence wasn't usually the answer, but in this instance, they had no choice. Neither of them was going down without a fight.

Both guys charged at the dupes, swinging weapons to try to pop them. They had to get rid of them all. And it seemed that *exploding* them was the only option to get the dupes off their backs.

When there were only a few dupes left, the two guys backed into each other, creating a power circle in the middle of the cave. "Back-to-back?" Isaiah asked, brandishing his weapon.

"Just like old times," James agreed.

"Huh?" Isaiah asked, glancing at his best friend.

"I don't know." James shrugged. "I was just *yes-and*ing you."

They punched, kicked, and swung their way through the remaining dupes, popping each like a water-balloon explosion of goo when they connected with a dupe's head. When there was only one dupe left in the cave with them, the friends approached it together. "We good?" Isaiah checked, nudging his best friend in the shoulder.

"Yeah," James agreed. "We're good." Together, they stomped on the head of the final Dupe James with a satisfyingly goopy *pop*!

Surrounded by the sickening sweet smell of watermelon Jolly Ranchers, they knew this battle was finally over.

CHAPTER TWENTY-SEVEN

James was celebrating his newfound freedom with a massive pile of pancakes, eggs, and bacon at the Harbor Stop. Both he and Isaiah were still covered in Dupe James goo, but it was irrelevant—at least he had food, clean water, and freedom.

"Sooo . . ." Isabella said timidly, glancing at Margot. "I think it's time for us to call your mom."

"I don't know," Margot said.

"What's the deal?" Isabella spat. "This is—"

"My parents are separated, okay?"

"Really?" Isaiah asked, shooting her a look. "Why didn't you tell me?"

"Because I didn't want to believe it's real. And I don't want to talk to my mom, because I don't want to talk about any of this."

"We don't have to call her . . ." Isaiah said quickly, understanding what a delicate situation this was. He wasn't going to push Margot to do something she wasn't comfortable with. He had more respect for her than that, and he knew she'd do the same for him, despite their ups and downs since Halloween.

"Um, I was in a hole for a week," James said, stuffing another bite of pancake in his mouth. "Maybe we call her mom. Respectfully . . ."

With a sigh, Margot pulled out her cell and dialed her mom in Seattle. "Hey, Mom, okay . . . some really scary stuff has been happening, and it has to do with a kid you went to school with named Harold Biddle—"

Margot's mom immediately cut her off when she heard the name. A name she'd tried to forget. A name that had haunted her for *years*. "Okay, listen to me," she told Margot. "This is important. Do not talk to anyone else about this. You can't trust any of the other parents. I'll be there as soon as I can."

Meanwhile, across town in the Biddle house, Nathan was hard at work doing Harold Biddle's bidding. He was quickly flipping through Harold's old scrapbook, crossing out pictures of people from his past.

First, he made an X through a picture of young Ben.

Then, he crossed out young Victoria, next to a drawing of his beloved mask.

Finally, he turned the page and made an X through young Eliza next to a drawing of the cuckoo clock.

Hearing a rustling behind him, Biddle-Bratt turned to see who'd entered the basement.

It was another Dupe James—come to finish the job that had been started at Harold's request. "Not all of us made it," Dupe

James told Biddle-Bratt. "But we found what you were looking for."

Biddle-Bratt grabbed the old suitcase from Dupe James's hand and set it gently atop his desk. "My old friend," he crooned, caressing the outside of the case. "Finally. I've been waiting for you."

He carefully snapped open the case—and screamed in torment. For where his best friend should have been, there was merely a shadowed outline. An empty space. A hole. "Where is he?" Bratt screamed in rage. "WHERE. IS. HE?!" Furious, he spun around and tossed the tragically empty case straight into Dupe James, sending goop flying everywhere within the dark and dusty Biddle basement.

PART FOUR

— *Lucas* —

GO EAT WORMS

CHAPTER TWENTY-EIGHT

Lucas only had one way left to connect with his dad—through stunts. That rush of adrenaline was the only thing that made him forget his dad was dead. And doing tricks like his dad had done was the only way to feel like his dad was still a part of his life.

"Lucas here," he narrated into his phone camera as he straddled his motorbike before school. Lucas was standing atop the mountain just above the spot where his dad had died. "Gonna do a little thing I like to call 'conquering the Booms of Doom.' Time for a Denn-defying stunt."

He'd been trying to muster up the courage to complete the very stunt that had taken the life of his dad, Dennis. Lucas would ride his bike off the Booms of Doom, but unlike the fate that had befallen his dad, *he* would survive.

He pressed two fingers to the sky as a salute to his pop, then revved the engine and shot toward the edge of the cliff. Lucas paused. It was a long way down. Lucas took a step backward. "Wind's not right," he said, then spun around to wheel his bike back home. He hated that he wasn't living up to his dad's reputation and restoring his honor, but he couldn't go through with it—not today, anyway.

At the bottom of the mountain, he rolled his bike back into the shed outside his apartment. Inside the dusty old space, he scanned the shelves loaded with various stunt gear—bikes, skateboards, and heaps of "Denniz Da Menaz" merch. His dad had been his hero, and Lucas wanted nothing more than to live his life like his dad had: fearlessly.

As Lucas lifted his bike onto the rack, he accidentally knocked over a box with some of his parents' old stuff from high school. Bending down, he scooped up a little glass eyeball. He palmed it, then tossed it into his pocket; that would make a sick accessory. It would be nice to wear something that had probably been his dad's at some point in time.

Just as Lucas stepped out of the shed, he spotted a car pulling up in front of the place he had shared with his mom since his dad died. It was the school guidance counselor, Mr. Stokes. Lucas was just about to wave hello when he noticed his mom was in the front seat of his counselor's car. Then, to his horror, his mom leaned across the car and *kissed* Mr. Stokes. *Whoa*. Lucas gulped. He flipped on his camera and caught the action on film. He wasn't sure what he was going to do with it, but he wanted proof he'd actually seen what he had just seen. Because this was *messed up*.

Once his mom was settled in at work a short while later, Lucas headed in to confront her. Surely she'd tell him what was going on. "Hey, mom," he said, adjusting the DENNIZ DA MENAZ hat he'd slipped onto his head after that morning's outing. "Where were you this morning?"

"Had to get down to the shop early to make some pies," she answered, refusing to meet his eye. Finally, she glanced up at him with a quick smile and said, "Oh! I haven't seen that hat in a while."

"Yeah, I found it when I was organizing the shed," he explained.

"Don't you think you're spending too much time in the shed?" she asked. "I know you miss your dad, but—"

"Someone has to," Lucas said, cutting her off. Sometimes it felt like he was the only one who missed his dad. Didn't his mom miss him, too? Why didn't they talk about him anymore?

Nora snapped her head up. "What does that mean?"

"I just want to keep dad's memory alive," he said. "One day, I'm gonna have swag with my own logo on it."

Nora shook her head. "Hopefully it will be advertising your *safe* accounting firm, though." When he didn't laugh, she gave him another look. "You okay?"

"Yeah." Lucas shrugged, then headed out to school with one of his mom's famous breakfast burritos in his hand. Even on a bad day, and even when she was really irritating him, these were always his favorite.

At school, Lucas was walking down the hall when Mr. Bratt stopped him. The new English teacher grabbed his shoulder and spun him around, glaring at the eyeball Lucas had found that morning. He'd attached it to his backpack, sort of like a lucky charm. "Hey!" he said, shaking Mr. Bratt's arm off him.

"Where did you get that?" Mr. Bratt snarled, gesturing to the eyeball.

Lucas stepped backward with his hands up. "Whoa, dude. No fly zone."

Mr. Bratt was acting like a nutter. "Where did you find it?" he growled.

"I don't know," Lucas said, trying to back away. "Around. Anyway, I'm late for class."

"What's your name again?" Mr. Bratt called after him as Lucas scuttled away.

"Lucas Parker!"

Mr. Bratt went still. *Parker*. That was a name he knew all too well. Then he grinned to himself as he realized something important. "Nora has him."

CHAPTER TWENTY-NINE

Isabella and James were chilling at a table in the corner of the library, waiting for the others to join them so they could talk through their plan. "I miss being bored," James whined.

"I would *kill* to be bored," Isabella said.

"I way prefer being bored to having a constant feeling of dread," James pointed to his chest. "Right here. At all times."

Isabella said, "I used to spend my days being jealous of Allison's terrible singing voice and hating my mom. I just want to get back to that."

James laughed, which made Isabella smile. After everything they'd gone through over the past week, Isabella was feeling like part of a group—finally. It felt good to have a place where she belonged, with people who were nice to her.

"I never knew you were funny," James said, still chuckling.

Isabella deadpanned, "I wasn't joking."

Isaiah sauntered over and tossed his bag on a chair. "I don't even know why we're at school today."

"At least we won't be alone when there's a zombie attack? Poltergeist? Werewolves? Just spitballing here," James said.

"It's truly insane that we're supposed to go about our day, pretending everything is okay," Isabella said.

"I know," Isaiah agreed. "But we just have to wait until Margot's mom gets here and tells us what's going on."

"When *is* Margot's mom coming?" Isabella asked.

Margot walked up just then and said, "I have no idea. If I'm being honest, I've been waiting a while for her to come back, which got me thinking."

"Oh no," James groaned.

"What if we told my *dad* . . . ?" Margot suggested. The other three looked at her as if she'd lost her mind. She went on to explain, "C'mon. We need to talk to someone old enough to pay taxes. I tell my dad everything. And he tells me everything. He never lies. He's like the most honest, normal person on the planet. There's no way he's involved in any of this."

"I've lived next door for a long time," Isaiah said, vouching for her. "He's like the OG of norm-core."

"His aura is beige," Margot went on. "He did puzzles *before* COVID."

Everyone nodded, seeing her point. They all knew they needed to tell some adult, and Margot's dad did seem like a good option. "What the hell," James said finally. "How much worse can this get?"

Isabella sighed. "Well, it always gets worse when someone asks that!"

After school, Lucas hunted down Margot at her locker. "Hey, Margot," he said, sounding more serious than she'd ever heard him. Lucas was always goofing around, being a joker who played everything off like it was all part of a complicated stunt. This was something completely different. "Can we talk?"

"Is this about what happened to you outside the Harbor Stop the other night?" Margot asked. Lucas had been knocked out when the troll—Isabella—had finally shown its face. She'd been wondering how much he knew about what had actually happened and how much danger he'd been in before she and Isaiah arrived to save him. "I've been meaning to fill you in on everything—"

"No," Lucas cut her off. "It's about us. I need you to come to my bedroom." She shot him a look. "That came out wrong. I need to show you something in my bedroom—no, still wrong. Look, just please come with me." Lucas sighed, noticing that she was still looking at him like some kind of psychopath. "I'm not going to murder you."

"Your pickup skills need work," Margot informed him.

"This is serious," he said.

"Okay." Margot shrugged. "Let's go."

When they got to Lucas and Nora's small apartment above the Harbor Stop, Lucas led her up the stairs to his room. Inside his bedroom, Margot took a quick look around. It was a little messy but very clearly showcased Lucas's personality. The walls were full of posters highlighting his BMX and skateboard heroes, including a large one of his dad mid-stunt. There were also posters of bands and family photos of Nora, Dennis, and Lucas at various ages throughout his life. Until recently, when the family-of-three photos ended for good. "Nice room," Margot noted. "It's not as . . . musky as most boys' rooms."

"Call me crazy, but I believe in good hygiene."

"I hope you don't take this the wrong way," Margot said, "but that's oddly surprising."

Lucas grinned. "I know, right?" Then he grew serious. "You should sit. This is going to be a little bit intense. I'm sorry."

Margot was unnerved by his expression. She sat, then Lucas held his phone in front of her face. She squinted and leaned in toward the screen. She watched, horrified, as she saw her dad and Nora, kissing, inside her dad's car. "What . . . what is this? That's my dad. And your . . ."

"Yeah, it's my mom. It's from this morning. He dropped her off."

"I can't believe he'd do this to my mom," Margot said, shaking her head. She couldn't *believe* this. Her mom was gone a lot lately, but her parents were still married. Her mom was still her *mom*! And her dad was, well, he was her dad. Her boring, vanilla, do-nothing-wrong dad, who was apparently a *cheater*.

"I'm sorry," Lucas said.

"Do they know that you know?"

"No." Lucas shook his head. "I gave my mom a chance to tell me the truth, but she lied to my face."

"I thought my dad just left before me this morning, but I guess maybe he never came home . . ."

"I'm sorry I had to be the one to tell you, but I thought you should know." Lucas studied her expression. "If it makes you feel better, my dad is dead."

She glanced at him. "It doesn't, but thank you."

"Hey, let me show you something else." He ran over to his glass terrarium, slid the top off, and reached inside. "These are my friends." Hundreds of worms squiggled and moved around his hand, but Lucas grabbed just one out of the bunch and dangled it in midair. "Want to see me eat one?" he asked, trying to lighten the mood.

"Ugh, no. Gross."

He dangled it over his face, playing with her. But then, suddenly, the worm got too close and shot straight up his nose! Lucas choked, trying to swallow or cough it back up. He could feel it wiggling in the cavities behind his face before, eventually, he managed to swallow it down—gone.

"Are you okay?" Margot asked, horrified.

"Yep, yep. It's all good."

"All good? Do you even know what kind of worm you just swallowed? What if it's a parasite?"

Lucas put a hand on his stomach. "It's protein now."

Margot shook her head. "And with that . . . I should go."

"Yeah." Lucas nodded. "I get it. I'll walk you home."

When Margot and Lucas strolled up to Margot's house, Isaiah was hanging around outside his own house. He looked at Lucas curiously. Why was *he* here? "You're bringing him to this thing with your dad?"

"What thing?" Lucas asked Margot.

"Change of plans," Margot told Isaiah. "I'm not talking to my dad about anything, ever again."

"Uh, what is going on?" Isaiah asked, wondering what had changed since that morning.

"What's going on is that we can't trust my dad," she told him.

Just then, Colin came out of the house with a bag of trash, wearing an apron that read CHEF DAD. He stopped and looked over at Margot and her friends. "Oh, hey . . . Lucas," Colin said, waving dorkily. "And Isaiah. I just got a new eight-thousand-piece puzzle of the Milky Way, if anyone's interested. No pressure."

No one replied. Margot just headed toward her front door, where her dad grinned at her and said, "So you're friends with Lucas Parker now, huh? That's unexpected. But good for you guys! Fun."

Outside, Isaiah and Lucas looked at each other awkwardly. Suddenly, Lucas's stomach let out the loudest, most intense, growling gurgle Isaiah had ever heard. He cringed, then clocked Lucas's facial expression. The dude looked like he was in serious pain.

"I don't feel good," Lucas said, turning to run. It felt like his entire intestines were wriggling around in his gut. "I gotta get home, like, now."

Isaiah waved him off. "Yeah, I can only go at my house, too. Say no more!"

CHAPTER THIRTY

That night, while Lucas was fast asleep, his "pets" made their move. Under the cover of darkness, the collection of worms inside Lucas's terrarium began to pulsate. En masse, they formed a squirming column, reaching up as one to open the lid of the terrarium. With a push of wriggling force, the mass came spilling out. They streamed up the sides of Lucas's bed, swarming over his sleeping body. While Lucas slumbered peacefully, the worms slithered into his nostrils, ears, and mouth—one by one, until every last worm had burrowed itself *inside* Lucas's body.

In the morning, Lucas woke up around his usual time. While he got dressed for the day, something felt a bit off, but he chalked it up to nerves, or restlessness, or one of the other things that made him constantly itch for thrills, like his dad.

As he passed his terrarium, he noticed that the lid was open. Rifling through the dirt inside, he was surprised to find the tank empty. Lucas shook his head, confused. How, exactly, does someone lose a giant cluster of worms?

From downstairs, his mom called to him, "Lucas! Breakfast!"

Lucas headed for the door, bumping into the frame of his bed on the way out of his room. But for once, he didn't feel the pain as he knocked into the wooden rail. He carried on, ready to face the day. Downstairs his mom handed him his usual breakfast burrito as he raced for the door. But as soon as he got outside the Harbor Stop and took a bite of his favorite meal, Lucas blanched. The burrito tasted like crap. He spit the bite out on the ground, then rounded the corner to toss the rest into the giant trash bin on the side of the building.

Just as he tossed the burrito in, Lucas got a whiff of the inside of the bin. It smelled oddly . . . incredible. He reached in, scooped up some of the rotten food and mess inside, and shoved it into his mouth. It tasted so good, Lucas couldn't help but reach in for more.

When he got to school, Lucas was descending the central staircase when someone knocked into him and he fell down a few steps. "Oh, dude!" the guy called out, looking down at where Lucas had landed. "You okay?"

Lucas stood and shook himself off. He'd fallen hard, but he was seemingly fine. "Yeah, I'm good."

"Really?" the dude said, cringing. "I totally nailed you."

Lucas shrugged. "Barely felt it." He shook himself off. He really hadn't felt anything. That was weird. He knew pain all too well from all his stunts and was surprised the fall had elicited *nothing*. Opening his locker, Lucas decided to try something: He slammed his hand against the door of the locker. Still nothing. It was almost as though his nerves had short-circuited. "Weird," he mused. Next, he held his hand between his locker door and the frame, then slammed it closed. The metal crunched loudly into bone with a sickening clang. Lucas popped the door back open again and pulled out his mangled hand and fingers, a drip of blood sliding down his wrist. His fingers were smashed, crooked, and obviously broken— but still, there was no pain.

A classmate walked past, getting a look at Lucas's bashed hand. "I'm going to throw up now," she said, holding her hand over her mouth.

"It's cool," Lucas said, wriggling his fingers. "I didn't feel it." Suddenly, his hand began to fix itself. There was a strange slithering sound inside Lucas's head as his busted hand began to crack and pop back into place. He strolled down the hall, marveling at whatever crazy stuff was going on within his body.

"Hey," Margot said, catching up to him. "Yesterday was, um, pretty sucky. How are you handling it?"

"Just kinda rolling with the punches," Lucas said. "And it's working."

Margot tilted her head. "Really? So you're okay?"

"Margs," Lucas said, acting all casual. "Listen."

"No one calls me Margs."

"I know you're in pain," he went on. "And I was, too. The thing about pain is you can choose to just not feel it."

"I don't think that's true."

Lucas grinned at her. "What I'm finding out today, though, is that it is."

CHAPTER THIRTY-ONE

That afternoon in study hall, Isaiah, Isabella, and James were in a heated discussion when Margot slid into a chair at the table with them. "She saw something in the forest the night of the party," Isaiah was saying. "It could be connected."

"But she sucks," Isabella cut in. "And she's rude. No offense."

"Who are we talking about?" Margot asked.

"Isaiah wants to bring Allison in on the *Haunted Housewives of Port Lawrence*," James explained.

"Yeah, no," Margot said, shaking her head. "Bad idea."

"I knew you would say that," Isaiah said. "What is your problem with her?"

Margot rolled her eyes. Wasn't it obvious? "We don't have enough time."

Isabella looked from Isaiah to Margot and back again. "What is *this* dynamic?" she asked. "Did you guys date at some point?"

"No!" Margot said at the same time Isaiah said, "We're neighbors."

"Neighbors who dated?" Isabella clarified.

"It's more like they're an old divorced couple, but now that they've retired and the kids are in college, they've finally entered the amicable part of their separation," explained James.

"No—" Isaiah began.

"Well, I'm feeling the vibes," Isabella said a little too casually.

"What vibes?" Allison asked, suddenly popping up beside their table. She looked pointedly at Isaiah. "Why did you ask me to come here?"

"We want to talk to you about what happened," he told her.

"No, we don't," Isabella whispered under her breath.

"What do you mean, 'what happened'?" Allison asked.

"In the forest," Isabella said.

"Nothing happened in the forest," Allison said shrilly, barely containing the panic that flashed across her face.

Margot leaned in to whisper to Isaiah, "Don't tell her."

Suddenly, Allison's expression shifted from fear to anger. She snapped back, "How about you don't tell my boyfriend what he should and shouldn't tell me?" Then she stormed off, forcing Isaiah to chase after her.

"I told you she sucks," Isabella muttered as soon as they were out of hearing range.

Out in the hall, Isaiah called after his girlfriend. "Allison, wait."

"Just tell me what's going on," Allison said, spinning around to confront him.

"That's what I've been trying to do!"

"Not your stupid ghost story," she protested. "I'm talking about with Margot. You guys have some kind of secret thing that I'm not in on."

"You want to know our secret?" Isaiah asked. "She helped me cheat on my test, so I could get a good enough grade to play in the game the night I broke my arm. That's it. That's our secret! You happy?"

Allison sneered. "That's supposed to make me feel better? A girl I've always suspected you had feelings for helped you *cheat* on a test? Maybe you're not as smart as I thought you were." Allison stormed away—again.

"Yeah!" Isaiah called after her. "That's why I cheated on the test!"

Suddenly, he heard the rev of a motorbike coming from somewhere nearby. What the—?

"What's up, dude?" It was Lucas, pushing his bike past Isaiah along the inclined floor of the hallway.

After school, Isaiah caught up to Margot, Isabella, and James. "Hey," he said. "Have you guys seen Lucas today?"

"Earlier today, I guess." James shrugged. "He's not one of the guys I keep track of, like Sam or . . . I guess I just keep track of Sam."

"Dude has been acting really weird," Isaiah said. "He was walking his motorbike through the hallway earlier."

"A lot's been going on with him," Margot explained.

"Seems like it," Isaiah said. "Last night he got pretty sick. After you went inside."

"I thought our meeting with Margot's dad was canceled?" James asked.

"It was," Margot said. "Lucas was just walking me home after he ate a worm—long story."

"So he finally ate that worm?" Isaiah laughed. "Dude was threatening to do that at the Halloween party."

Margot stopped walking suddenly. "Right," she said, something clicking into place. "He found those worms at the Biddle house. Camera, mask, dupes . . ."

"Worms!" the other three said in unison.

"This is bad," Margot said with a groan.

Suddenly, Margot's dad appeared in the hallway. He gestured for her to follow him, which was annoying, but her dad looked pretty serious.

Inside his office, she asked, "What's going on?"

"I know about everything," Colin said.

"Everything?" Margot blanched. "Who told you?"

"That doesn't matter right now. What matters is that I'm the guidance counselor at this school, and my own daughter has been accused of cheating."

"Wait, what?" Margot said, her mouth falling open. Who knew about what she and Isaiah had done during that test? Only her . . . and Isaiah. How could her dad have found out?

"Did you give your test answers to Isaiah?" her dad asked, point-blank. "Did he pressure you? This is completely out of character. Margot, did you cheat?"

She looked at him and admitted, "I did. I guess it runs in the family." Her dad looked at her, totally confused. "I know about you and Nora."

"Where did you—"

"Were you just planning never to tell me or Mom?" she snapped.

"It's not that simple," her dad said feebly.

"Honestly, it is pretty simple. You're sleeping with someone who isn't your wife!"

Suddenly, there was a commotion outside Colin's window. Both of them jumped up and ran outside. In the parking lot, a crowd had gathered, and they were all staring up, looking toward the roof of the school.

Margot and Colin looked in the same direction as everyone else to find Lucas poised astride his motorbike, clearly planning to ride off the roof to the ground. "Lucas!" Margot screamed. "What are you doing?"

Colin waved, trying to get his attention. "Lucas! Get down from there this instant!"

Isaiah was standing next to Isabella and James outside. All three of them were looking up, watching to see how this played out. "Well," Isaiah said slowly. "This has to be Harold."

"Is it, though?" James asked. "Because Lucas does crazy stuff like this all the time."

Just then, Lucas revved the bike's engine. With one final, reckless grin, he rode straight off the roof and landed directly on Colin's car—crushing the whole front hood, but sticking his landing.

Colin ran out to him, surprised Lucas had survived the stunt. "I have had just about enough of you! Your antics and stunts are out of control. I'm going to recommend expulsion to Principal Stroller."

Lucas smirked back at him. "And I'm going to recommend you stop banging my mom." He stormed away, leaving Colin staring after him.

Margot chased after Lucas, and when she caught up, she could see that his arm wasn't hanging like it normally did. It seemed to be out of its socket. "Lucas, stop. You should go to the hospital to get that checked out. Your shoulder doesn't look right."

He touched his arm, and as if by some kind of magic, it suddenly popped back into its socket. "Hospital?" he asked her. "Why would I go to the hospital? I'm invincible."

Margot suddenly noticed that Lucas's skin seemed to be crawling. "Lucas," she asked him, "what's under your skin?"

"I wish I could stay and talk," Lucas said, not answering her question. "But I have a Denn-defying date with the Booms of Doom."

CHAPTER THIRTY-TWO

"We need to talk!" Margot said, running into the Harbor Stop shortly afterward.

Nora nodded. "Your father called and filled me in. I know how difficult this must be for you—"

"It's not about your stupid affair. I'm here about Lucas! I think Harold got to him, in the form of worms."

"Worms?"

"He found them at that Halloween party. And then he ate one last night. I think they're crawling inside him, and I'm worried he's about to get badly hurt," Margot said in a rush. "He mentioned the Booms of Doom, and then he rode off on his motorbike."

The blood drained from Nora's face. She grabbed her jacket and keys, then raced out of the shop.

"What are the Booms of Doom?" Margot asked, chasing after her.

"It's where his dad died," Nora explained. "Get in."

When they reached the Booms of Doom, Nora and Margot found Lucas perched at the edge of the tall cliff. "Time for a

Denn-defying stunt," he was reciting over and over again. He put his foot on the pedal, ready to kick the engine into gear.

But Nora slammed on the brakes and raced out of her car, screaming, "Lucas! No!"

"It's okay," Lucas said with a smile. "I've got this. I don't feel anything—no pain, no hurt, no problem."

"It's the worms, Lucas," Margot told him. "They're tricking you."

"No, they're helping me fulfill Dad's legacy." The worms writhed and wriggled under Lucas's skin, urging him on.

"Lucas," Nora said, stepping in front of his bike. "I know how much you want to feel close to your dad. But this isn't the way."

Lucas shook his head. "Yes, it is. We were a team. Father and son. He wanted me to be just like him." He kicked the pedal, revving the bike's engine. "Move out of my way, or I'll run you over."

"No," Nora said, refusing to budge. "I know you're mixed up and confused right now, but you need to know: This was not a run your dad did because he thought he could make it." Lucas eyed her warily, the worms moving faster and more urgently under his skin. "He did it because he knew he *couldn't*." Nora waited for this to register. "He left a note. I didn't tell you because you idolized him so much, and I didn't want to ruin that for you. But you need to hear the truth."

"No!" Lucas screamed. This couldn't be true.

"He wanted to die," Nora said gently. "And this was his way of doing it."

Lucas stepped off the bike, letting it fall to the ground as he struggled to fight against the worms who were urging him to go for it—to make the run. Suddenly, Lucas's whole body convulsed, and he bent in half involuntarily. The worms inside him came rushing out in a tidal wave, thousands upon thousands of worms retching out of him onto the ground.

"I'm sorry," Nora said, rushing to his side as the worms burrowed into the dirt—disappearing from sight. "I should have told you. I shouldn't have kept his secret."

Lucas sobbed. "I miss him, Mom. I miss him so much."

"I know you do," Nora said, rubbing his back. "I miss him, too."

Suddenly, the ground beneath them began to shake. Nora and Lucas broke apart and spun around, just in time to see a wave of worms pouring back out of the dirt as one giant mass. They'd somehow banded together and formed a giant, horrifying monster worm that towered over the three of them. The head of the worm monster tracked Lucas as he stepped cautiously backward, attempting to protect his mom and Margot from the beast. "They want me back," he realized, just as a tendril of worms erupted out of the mass and shot toward Lucas like a lasso.

He knew he had to lead the worms away, to keep his mom and Margot safe. The worms wanted him and him alone. He hopped back on his bike, kicked the engine, and rode off the edge of the Booms of Doom. The giant worm monster followed, slithering down the steep path after him. At the bottom of the run, Lucas could see the lip of the embankment that would send him up and into the air, launching him onto the floating log booms. This was the jump that killed his father.

At the last second, Lucas twisted his handlebars and slid right, avoiding the jump altogether. He wanted a different fate than his dad's. He raced down the fire road, heading for the old lumber mill. Gunning the bike, he was able to stay just ahead of the worms, but not by much. They had power and speed, and they seemed to be gaining on him every second. As it pursued him, the worm monster knocked logs loose, sending them scattering onto the road like a child's building blocks. Nothing seemed capable of stopping it. But Lucas had an idea.

As they chased after Lucas and the monster in Nora's car, Margot yelled, "You know this has to do with Harold."

Nora shot her a look. She knew. The car reached the old lumber mill at the same time that Lucas arrived on his bike. "Inside!" Lucas screamed to them, blasting open the doors to the old lumber mill with the front tire of his bike. As soon as they were all safely inside, Lucas slammed the doors closed. Angry, the giant worm rammed into the side of the building. It was clear they wouldn't be able to hold it off for long. That worm was getting in; it was just a question of *when*.

"Mom, get the sawmill on," Lucas instructed. "I'll buy us time."

The worms had split up to crawl under the doors and through the windows of the old building, but now they were reforming and rebuilding into swirling tendrils of monster yet again. Just as Lucas revved his bike's engine, the door to the lumber mill burst open and the remaining worms flooded inside to become the massive beast once more.

Lucas sped away, leading the monster into the heart of the

warehouse. Meanwhile, Nora grabbed Margot's arm and pulled her toward the metal stairs. She was heading for the control room to turn on the machinery so she could help her son act out his plan. "Which button turns on the chipper?" Nora asked, watching through the windows of the control room as Lucas led the monster in that direction. They didn't have much time. The two of them flicked at buttons, trying to find the one that could do the most damage, the one that would flip on the chipper and hopefully help this story end the way they wanted it to.

Finally, the blades of the wood chipper roared to life. Lucas zipped forward, getting as close to the mouth of the chipper as he dared. Then, at the last possible second, he squeezed his hand brake and flew into a front wheelie. The giant worm bore down on him, nearly consuming the bike and Lucas. But before it could wrap itself around his body fully, Lucas leaped up and grabbed the top railing above the mouth of the machine.

The giant worm monster and Lucas's bike were pulled together into the funnel, then spit into the metal blades. In a split second, the giant machine created mincemeat out of both bike and beast. Lucas hung on, dangling from the mouth of the chipper as the machine spit gallons of worm-slaw out the other end. It was over.

"What happened here?" a police officer asked Nora, once they'd all collected themselves and Lucas and Margot had been taken home in James's Jeep.

"I'm so sick of lying," Nora said, feeling the exhaustion from the day and the *years* hanging over her like a wet blanket. "I'm going to tell you what *really* happened." She began to recount the story—the worms, the ghost of Harold Biddle, and all the other weird stuff that had been happening. She spilled it all, but she never imagined the story would seem so unbelievable that it would land her in the psychiatric ward of the hospital. Unfortunately, that's exactly what happened, just like it had thirty years ago.

Why wouldn't anyone ever believe her? Why weren't the others willing to talk? Why did they always try to shut her up and pretend none of it had happened? Nora was frustrated, and now, thanks to Isabella's mom, her old friend Victoria, she was also highly medicated, too. So medicated by her doctor friend that she could hardly keep her head up, could hardly think, let alone explain anything.

"I just want to know when I can talk to my son," Nora pleaded, taking the meds the nurse forced on her. But no one would let her talk to Lucas, no one would give her any answers at all. The only thing anyone would give her were more meds. Victoria just kept shoving pills at her, trying to keep her quiet.

As she wandered into the ward's rec room, Nora looked up in a daze. She stumbled, then scrambled backward again. A burned, charred Harold Biddle was staring at her from across the room. "I want him back!" Biddle yelled. Nora screamed, terrified.

She had no doubt about it: The past had come back to haunt them all.

READER
BEWARE

CHAPTER THIRTY-THREE

"This is everything?" Mr. Stokes asked, tossing Lucas's bag into the trunk of his car.

"I like to travel light," Lucas said with a shrug. While his mom was stuck in the hospital, he was stuck staying with Margot and her dad. As if *that* wasn't awkward, given everything that was happening between Nora and Colin.

"You're welcome to stay with us as long as Nora needs," Colin said, offering him a kind smile as they pulled up to the house.

When she showed him to the guest room, Margot asked Lucas, "Are you okay? I mean . . . it's a lot. All of this is."

"Yeah," Lucas said, flopping down on his new loaner bed. "I just wish I could visit my mom. Your dad said it was about being a minor, but I bet I'm the one person she actually wants to see. That's messed up." Lucas looked around the room, then glanced at Margot. "This is super weird, right? I mean, our parents are . . . hooking up. A ghost is haunting us for some reason. And now I'm, like, sleeping over?"

"I'm glad it's you," Margot told him. "I mean, I'm glad it's you that's here. I mean—"

"I'm glad I'm here, too." Lucas glanced at her, trying not to act like the idiot he always became when he was around Margot. A different kind of idiot than the one who rode skateboards and motorbikes off buildings.

Margot shrugged. "At least it can't get any more awkward, right?"

As if on cue, the doorbell rang. Margot walked over to the window and peeked outside, checking to see who was there. She turned around, looking shocked. "It's my mom."

That night at dinner, Margot's mom, Sarah, took her usual seat at the head of the table. Though she hadn't been home in weeks, some habits die hard. "So . . ." Lucas said, trying to make conversation and break the tension in the room. "You live in Seattle now? Like, permanently?"

"Oh no," Sarah said, taking a small bite. "It was temporary. I'm back now."

Lucas stole a glance at Colin, who looked shocked by this news.

"You're back?" Margot asked, sounding just as surprised as Colin looked.

"*Back* back?" Colin repeated.

"I wanted to tell you in person," Sarah explained. "I thought it would be a fun surprise."

"Very fun," Colin said, forcing a smile. "Very, very fun."

Lucas looked from Colin to Sarah to Margot. He wondered if *his* mom had any idea *Margot's* mom was back; that was gonna make things with her and Mr. Stokes—Colin—quite awkward. Truth be told, none of this seemed very *fun* at all.

When Margot's dad stepped away from the table to grab some wine, Margot leaned in toward her mom. "So, what's going on? We haven't talked to any of the other parents, like you asked. We've been waiting on you. So . . . tell us."

"I can't get into this now," Sarah said in a hush. "There are some things I have to take care of first—"

"Are you serious?" Margot growled.

"You cannot imagine how complicated this is," Sarah said as if that were any kind of real explanation.

"Um, yes we can!" Margot argued. The ghost of Harold Biddle had gone after every single one of her friends—she could definitely understand how complicated this was.

As soon as Colin was back at the table, he clocked the tension between mother and daughter. "What are we talking about?" he asked casually.

"Nothing, as usual," Margot snapped, pushing her chair back. "Can I be excused?" Then, without waiting for an answer she turned and stormed away from the table.

On the other side of town, Isaiah was heading across the parking lot after his physical therapy session with the athletic trainer when Allison caught up to him.

"What are you doing here?" Isaiah asked her.

"You're avoiding me," Allison said, gingerly putting her hand on his good arm. "So I came to you."

Isaiah pulled out the keys to his dad's car. He sighed. "You were the one who told Colin about Margot cheating on the test."

"She deserved it," Allison pointed out. Margot was always acting so high-and-mighty; she deserved to be called out for cheating. Let everyone know she wasn't so perfect after all.

"Did I deserve it, too?" he asked. "Because now I'm going to be in trouble."

"He's not going to do anything about it," Allison scoffed. "Mr. Stokes is her dad."

Isaiah shook his head. He'd had it with Allison's drama. "You know, this isn't about Margot anymore. This is about you. And me. And how it's not working anymore."

"You think?" Allison spat. "Then have the guts to finish it."

"You're right," Isaiah said with a sigh. "I'm sorry, okay? We're done."

Allison glared back at him. With one final nod of her head, she agreed. "You're right. We are."

"So that's it," Isaiah told James later that night. "I ended it with Allison."

"Finally," James said, rolling his eyes.

"Hey," Isaiah said. "She wasn't the worst."

James laughed. "She wasn't even interesting enough to be the worst. This breakup was inevitable. Like a straight guy buying an ugly pair of pants." Growing more serious, James asked, "Have you told Margot yet?"

"No . . . I was planning on telling her when she gets here," Isaiah said. "You know, Lucas is staying at her house now." He peeked at James and asked nervously, "You don't think that's anything to worry about, do you?"

James shook his head. "Nah. Lucas is pretty straightforward . . . and very hot. And you have spent the last couple years telling everyone, including Margot, that she's your good pal and that you have no romantic feelings for her, even though you clearly do. So, no, I see no problems." He lifted his eyebrows. Isaiah was fooling *no one* when it came to his and Margot's "friendship."

Isabella arrived then, with a pizza. "Crisis makes me hungry," she told the other two. "Margot's still not here. Isn't this *her* meeting?"

Margot wasn't there because she was too busy steaming about her mom. "She goes off to Seattle," she ranted as she and Lucas strolled toward James's house. "And doesn't tell me why, fine. She never tells me anything. But there are objects literally *haunting* us that she clearly knows something about! So, it really is not fine. This is the one time she could actually come through for me, but no."

"She's a mystery," Lucas said, shrugging.

"Not in a good way. She's been so distant since I started high school, as if she's done with me."

"Maybe she just hates hanging out with teenagers," Lucas suggested as they turned a corner.

"Or just . . . me."

Lucas looked at her seriously. "That's not possible." He locked eyes with Margot, hoping she understood that—for once—he was being totally serious. Margot was amazing, and he wanted to be the one who made her believe it.

Margot grinned, then looked around to figure out where they were. They'd been walking for a while now, but they didn't appear to be any closer to James's house than when they'd left hers. "Is this the way to James's house?"

"It's the long way," Lucas said, a skip in his step. "I kinda wanted to show you something." He paused at the edge of a playground. "Ta-da!" Margot looked around, confused. "It doesn't look like much, but this is actually the spot where I've broken most of the bones in my body."

"And you're showing me this because . . ."

"Even when it feels totally hopeless, and you're hurting," Lucas told her earnestly, "eventually, things get better. And I just think maybe that was a good thing for you to know right now."

Margot smiled at him. There was a lot hidden beneath Lucas's goofy exterior; way more than she'd ever noticed before. "It probably is. Thanks. For taking me to the site of your broken bones. It means a lot."

There was a long pause. Finally, Lucas looked directly at her and said, "I think you're really cool, and so funny without trying to be. And so smart. And you make me feel dumb, but not in a mean way. I really want to kiss you, but I'm not gonna kiss you because it feels like—"

Margot studied him as he spoke. Lucas was *so* unlike anyone else she knew—direct and honest and open. Suddenly, Margot leaned forward and touched their lips together. It made things immediately feel a little better, at least for now.

"Sorry we're late!" Margot said as she and Lucas rushed into James's game room a little while later.

James immediately noticed Margot's smile was brighter than usual, and Lucas's cheeks were flushed. Isaiah couldn't help but pay attention to how *close* Margot and Lucas were standing.

"Where were you guys?" Isaiah asked.

Lucas brushed it off. "Took the long way."

"What did your mom say?" James asked, getting down to business.

"Kind of . . . nothing," Margot reported. "She gave me some line about not wanting to say the wrong thing. She did say 'yet,' though, so maybe later she'll tell us . . . something? Later?"

"So what do we do now?" James asked. "Just go to school? Wait for the next horrible thing to happen?"

Isabella sighed. "I think that's kind of our life right now."

CHAPTER THIRTY-FOUR

"You're drugging her?" Sarah demanded as she stormed into Victoria's office at the hospital the next afternoon.

"Keep your voice down," Victoria hissed. She gestured for her old high school friend to close the door to her office. "Nora is sedated because she was reported to be a danger to herself. Nora is under *my* care, Sarah. I'm her doctor."

"Oh, please," Sarah scoffed. As if this was *care*; this was self-preservation.

"*Oh, please?*" Victoria repeated. "You waltz back into town and think you can call the shots? Nora was at the sawmill talking about haunted worms. She's having a nervous breakdown! What do you think happens after someone says something like that to the police?"

"I'm supposed to believe that you think you're *helping* her?" Sarah accused.

"I'm trying to *handle* the situation," Victoria said. "She's agitated. Talking to the cops about ghosts. Where do you think that's going?"

Sarah met the other woman's eyes. "She said Biddle's back and that he's looking for *him*."

Victoria rolled her eyes. "That's exactly why she needs to be helped."

"Do you believe her?" Sarah asked. She wasn't sure what to believe, but she knew there was a lot more to this story than any of them could possibly understand, and it was clear that *something* was going on.

"Of course I don't," Victoria said with a sigh. Sarah wasn't entirely sure she believed Nora, either, but she could tell Victoria was deliberately trying to silence their old friend, no matter the cost. "This is too dangerous, Sarah. The lives we've built. Her life, too. All of it goes away if she can't keep it together. We all lose everything. Our jobs, our *kids*."

Sarah stormed out, heading back to the patient floor. What Victoria was doing wasn't right. And she couldn't cover up yet another wrong.

When she located Nora, she sat across from her old friend and reached out a hand to touch her gently. "Listen to me, Nora," she said. "You're not unwell. They just want you to think you are."

Nora looked at her blankly, her expression vacant. They had her so drugged up that she could barely even keep her eyes open.

"The medication they're giving you is for people who are seeing things that aren't there," Sarah explained. "But that isn't you. If you want to get out of here, you have to stop taking the pills and stop talking crazy. They don't understand. They don't believe you." She waited until Nora was looking right at her to add, "But I do. You're right. We need to protect our kids. We'll figure this out."

CHAPTER
THIRTY-FIVE

Inside the Biddle house, Nathan was tucked behind Harold's old desk, flipping through Harold's scrapbook. He looked up, catching the reflection in the mirror across the room. Harold stared back at him, his eyes hooded. "It's time for them to learn the truth," Harold's reflection told Nathan.

Nathan snapped the scrapbook closed and stood up, tucking it under his arm.

As soon as he got to school, Nathan located Margot in her usual spot in the library. Swooping up behind her, Nathan dropped the scrapbook on the table in front of her. It landed on the table with a loud *slap*, jolting Margot out of her thoughts. "Hey, Mr. Bratt," she said, looking up at him.

"Your mom's name is Sarah, right?" he asked, sounding slightly breathless.

"Yeah," Margot said, uneasy. "Why do you ask?"

"Well, I was cleaning out my basement and found this scrapbook."

"The Biddle basement?" Margot clarified.

"Yeah," Nathan said, his voice cheerful. "You should show it to your mom. I think there are some pictures of her from high school in there. I think she'll get a kick out of it." Then he paused and added, "You can look at it, too." He pushed it closer to her, then took off.

Nervously, Margot ran a hand across the slightly burnt cover of the scrapbook. Gingerly, she flipped through the pages, stopping on a page with a picture of her mom as a young teen. She stared at the photo, realizing her mom was sitting in this very library when the photograph had been taken.

Suddenly, Margot heard a voice. Spinning around, she realized she'd been transported into the past. Into the same scene she'd been looking at from the scrapbook.

"Hey, Harold!" Sarah said, waving at a kid sitting at a table across the library. It was Harold Biddle, and he was hunched over a scrapbook filled with photos, writing, and drawings. "Are you coming to photo club?"

"Yeah," Harold said, gathering up his things.

"See you in the darkroom in ten!" Sarah called, waving back at him.

Margot was shaken awake by the ancient librarian. "Are you okay? You've just been staring off into space."

Margot suddenly stood up, stunned by what she'd just witnessed. She looked down at the scrapbook. Had it actually *transported* her into the past? She flipped the page, noticing that the next scrapbook entry was titled "In a Darkroom," and it was covered in photographs of her mom's teenaged face. She jumped up and ran out of the library.

Stepping into the AV room, which had been the PLHS darkroom back in the nineties, Margot muttered to herself, "This is such a great idea. Nothing weird could possibly happen." She opened the book, and moments later, Margot was once again transported.

"Harold, these pictures are amazing," Sarah said, leaning over Harold's shoulder to see the photos he'd just developed—a picture of a cuckoo clock, a mask, a pile of worms.

"These are kind of, like, my favorite things," Harold said nervously.

"I know you said no," Sarah said suddenly. "But I think you should come and hang out with my friends this weekend." She paused, holding up a hand as Harold started to protest. "You're cooler than you think."

Suddenly, Margot was flipped back to the present when someone crashed their way into the AV room. "What are you doing in here?" the guy asked, studying her curiously.

Margot stared into space and whispered, "Harold and my mom were friends . . ."

The AV guy nodded. "Cool. Can I just get a projector?"

Margot raced to find her friends. This was nuts. She had to tell them what she'd discovered. "My mom knew Biddle!" she cried as soon as they were all together. She'd summoned everyone to meet her in the school auditorium, so she could try slipping into another scene and dive back into the truth of the past.

"What?" Isabella asked. "How do you know?"

"It's all in here." Margot held up the scrapbook. "If I'm in the location that the page is about, I see the vision. That's it. That's the way it works. All the information we need is in this scrapbook." She slammed it down, waiting for the others to react.

Finally, Isaiah said, "Is this the scrapbook that Mr. Bratt gave you?" He picked it up and said, "This ends badly. Trust me."

"I promise you," Margot said. "My mom is never going to tell us what's going on. This is the only way I'm going to find out the truth. I have to do this. I have to go back in." She flipped the pages of the old book until she came to a page with a drawing of theater masks on it. Then she sat down on the stage, stared at the page, and flipped back in time.

Harold Biddle paced anxiously on the stage, looking like he hadn't slept in days.

"Harold?" Sarah asked, crossing the stage to where her friend stood. "What's going on?"

"I'm scared," Harold told her, gripping her arms. "Really scared—"

"Scared of what? What's going on, Harold?" Sarah asked, her voice rising as Harold's eyes darted around the room.

"I think someone is trying to hurt me."

"Hurt you?" Sarah asked. "What does that mean, Harold? Did someone threaten you?"

"Yes. No. I can't explain it."

Sarah suddenly stepped backward, then said, "I have to go, okay? I'm sorry. We can talk about this later?" Harold grabbed her arm, squeezing so hard Sarah couldn't move. "Harold, what are you doing? Let go of my arm!"

"Please!" Harold begged. "Don't leave me!"

But Sarah somehow managed to pull her arm free, then ran away—clearly upset. Harold called after her, but she was gone. Suddenly, Harold spun around and looked across the stage. "You can't go either, Margot," he said. As he spoke, his skin began to blister, then erupted in flames. He transformed from a live person to a charred body, then said, "Come with me."

"Margot?" Isabella said, shaking her friend. But Margot's eyes were dead; her body completely lifeless. It was as though she was nothing more than a shell.

"What's happening?" Lucas asked, his voice panicked.

"Margot!" Isaiah screamed into her face. "Come on! Wake up!"

"I can't believe we let her do this," James wailed. "It's like we've learned nothing."

"She didn't give us a choice!" Isaiah pointed out.

Suddenly, Isabella slapped Margot across the face. The others spun around to glare at her. "What? I was trying to save her life."

James studied the scrapbook. "Okay, she said we have to be in the place that connects to the scrapbook page." He pointed. "The book flipped open to this page—that's the Biddle house."

"That's it," Lucas said, brightening. "That's how we get her out. We use the scrapbook at the Biddle house."

To get her to the car, they had to prop Margot's body on a dolly and cart her through the school hallways, pretending it was just a fun prank. A few people gave them weird looks, but James laughed them all off and blurted out, "Drama kids, am I right?"

Outside, they rolled her to James's Jeep and heaved her into the backseat, where they propped her body up between Isabella and Lucas for the ride to the Biddle house.

"Please, I don't understand," Margot said as the charred Biddle dragged her across the driveway at the Biddle house. "What do you want?"

Suddenly, a very alive, teen version of Harold came out of the house and onto the front steps. He looked around, curious, as if he were looking for something or someone, then headed back inside.

"What is this?" Margot asked, realizing she was still trapped in some sort of scrapbook memory.

Biddle's ghost pointed silently at the house, urging her to watch.

Suddenly, five masked teenagers raced around the edge of the house. They rushed through the side door of Harold's house and disappeared inside.

"Who are they?" Margot asked, but Ghost Biddle didn't answer—he just tightened his grip and dragged her through the front door to see for herself.

Inside, Margot watched as Harold lit a candle inside his darkened living room. For some reason, he looked terrified. He hustled to the basement door, slamming it closed behind him. A moment later, the five teens ran through the Biddle living room, toward the front door. Their footsteps pounded on the old wooden floorboards. From the other side of the basement door, Harold called out, "Stay away from me!"

A second later, Margot found herself standing on the other side of the basement door. Now she was holding a candle, and someone was rattling the knob on the other side of the door. In the next moment, Margot fell, rolling down the stairs, dropping the candle as she hit the carpet at the bottom. The whole room went up in flames, and Margot was choking, gasping on smoke, as the charred, ghostly form of Harold Biddle towered over her.

Just before she lost consciousness in the flames, Margot was being dragged up and out of smoke and fire by Isaiah and Lucas. At the top of the stairs, James and Isabella were waiting. They grabbed her and pulled her the rest of the way outside.

Outside, surrounded by her friends, Margot fell to her knees, coughing and gasping for air. As soon as she'd caught her breath, she said, "He followed me into the scrapbook. There were other people in the house."

Just then, all five of them turned as five masked figures ran out of the house, screaming at one another. They dropped their hoods, staring back at the house, which was now engulfed in flames.

"Mom?" Margot said, staring at a teen Sarah who was standing outside the house alongside four others.

"You found it?" Nora asked, revealing her own face.

"I found it," said Ben, pulling off his mask. He held up a case.

"Dad?" Isaiah said from where he stood across the yard with his own friends.

"We have to get him out!" Sarah screamed, charging toward the house.

Suddenly, flames spit out the basement window, shattering the glass. For a moment, the flames formed the face of Harold Biddle. But only Nora could see the outline, and she knew immediately what it meant. "He's gone," she told the others. "Harold's gone."

"No," Sarah sobbed. "This isn't real."

"I told you it was," Nora snapped at her. Lucas looked at his mom as she spoke to her friends. "You didn't believe me."

"Now what?" Victoria asked, and Isabella studied how her mom had looked and sounded as a teen. "Do we call someone?"

"No," Eliza told the others. James stared at his own mom as she added, "Harold's dead. Doesn't mean we have to ruin our lives, too. I can't go to jail. Grab the case."

Ben grabbed the case, and the five teens fled.

"You guys," James said as the five of them snapped back out of the scrapbook and into the real world. "Did we just find out our parents are murderers?"

"No," Margot said, shaking her head in disbelief. "This isn't possible."

"Why not?" Isabella scoffed. "It makes perfect sense. That's why all of this has been happening to us. The camera. The mask. The worms. Harold's making us pay for what our parents did to him. He's getting revenge."

"Oh my god," James said, clutching his hair. "We're murder nepo-babies."

Margot snapped, "They wouldn't just kill someone."

"Well, they literally just did," Lucas pointed out.

"Margot's right," Isaiah said. "There has to be more to this story. Like, what was in that case?"

Just then, Mr. Bratt strolled out of the front door of the modern-day Biddle house, holding the case they had just seen Ben holding in their vision from the past. "You want to know what's in the case?" he said. "Come inside. I'll tell you everything."

BEFORE

— *1925* —

EPHRAIM BRATT

CHAPTER THIRTY-SIX

*N*athan Bratt's great-grandfather was an aspiring magician named
Ephraim Bratt. Ephraim struggled to find success on the mean streets
of New York City, and he longed for the full houses and respect afforded to
other magicians and performers of the day. Desperate to find fame and fortune, Ephraim visited Madame Zelda, a purveyor of fine magical wares.
There was little to nothing he could afford, but he was desperate.

Just as he was about to leave the shop, Ephraim heard something calling to him from inside a case on a shelf. "Over here," *the voice called out.*

"What's that?" *Ephraim asked Madame Zelda, pointing.* "In that case."

"That puppet is cursed," *Madame Zelda told him.* "I think you
would not be so keen to possess it if you knew its dark tale." *She pulled the
case down and set it on the counter. Inside the case was a ventriloquist
dummy. Ephraim was immediately captivated and begged Madame Zelda
to tell him the dummy's secret.*

"In the old country," *she told him,* "long ago, there was a magician
named Kanduu who became obsessed with controlling others. He wanted
to become the puppet master of the entire town. But people feared him.
And they used his own magic to trap his evil soul inside this
puppet . . . crafted from coffin wood."

Ephraim was entranced. "Ooh," he said, rubbing a hand over the case. "Creepy. Can I use that story in my act?" He took the puppet home, despite the shop owner's warnings, and began to work with the dummy, whose name he learned was Slappy. One night, he noticed a card tucked into Slappy's suit coat. He plucked it out and began to read the words on the card aloud: "Karru Marri Odonna Loma Molonu Karrano?"

Though Ephraim didn't realize it immediately, he had uttered the very words Slappy needed to return to life. Slowly, Slappy began to control Ephraim's life, offering him the fame and success he'd always craved. But it would come at a cost. Ephraim became so obsessed with Slappy and their newfound fame that he soon chose spending time with the dummy over time with his family. It wasn't long before Slappy and Ephraim were alone—a dynamic duo, destined for greatness. Together. If only Ephraim had realized Slappy was the one in control of their act, and Ephraim was now little more than his puppet.

One night, Ephraim began to understand just how dangerous Slappy could be when he wasn't happy. When the manager of their act told them he was bringing in a new performer to share the stage with them, Slappy was furious. He wanted Ephraim to do something about this information—to keep anyone from pushing them aside and out of the spotlight. "You have no choice," Slappy told Ephraim when their manager came to speak with them about the changes.

Ephraim nodded at Slappy, understanding what he needed to do. He began reciting the curse that Slappy had told him would always allow him to maintain total control: "Adanna Meenu Sanara Kudarash."

Suddenly, the manager's face froze in place. Lines formed between the edges of his mouth and his nose, and within seconds, the transformation was complete. He'd been turned into a ventriloquist dummy.

Ephraim's manager had been Slappified.

After that, Ephraim grew frightened. What more was Slappy capable of? He'd never wanted to hurt anyone. He just wanted to find fame and fortune. But Slappy had bigger goals. He'd been trapped inside a doll for more years than he could count, and now he wanted to find an earthly body in which to live out his dreams again. Ephraim knew he had to do something to stop this from happening.

And so, he packed his dummy back up in his case, bought an old, remote hunting lodge in the woods, and set to work hiding Slappy from the world. Over his remaining years, Ephraim made it his mission to keep Slappy from hurting anyone else. He dug a hole in the basement wall of his new house and tucked Slappy away inside. But before he could close the hole up, sealing Slappy in forever with one final brick, he heard his dummy's voice call out from inside the case: "After all these years, I hoped you would change your mind, Ephraim. But I see that this is finally the end."

"I'm not going to let anyone find you, ever again," Ephraim vowed.

Just as Ephraim placed the final brick into place, entombing Slappy's case into the wall of his basement, Slappy muttered, "Oh, someone will find me . . ."

BEFORE

— *1993* —

HAROLD BIDDLE

CHAPTER THIRTY-SEVEN

Years later, not long after Ephraim Bratt had died, Harold Biddle and his parents—Perry and Georgia—were excited about moving into their lovely new house, a remote former hunting lodge nestled deep in the woods. They'd inherited the place from Georgia's reclusive grandfather, whom she'd never even met. Georgia was Ephraim Bratt's closest relative, and now the place was all theirs. It was now the Biddle house.

It was time for a fresh start in a small seaside town called Port Lawrence, where Harold's parents hoped he might finally find friends. Harold had always been a bit of a loner—with hobbies like worm-keeping, photography, and scrapbooking, it could be hard to fit in—but he longed for true friends.

"We're going to like it here," Perry promised his son as they walked into the house for the first time. "You're going to like it here."

"Kids are the same everywhere," Harold muttered.

"They aren't," Perry vowed. "I promise they aren't."

On Harold's first day of school, his parents presented him with a special gift that would allow him to capture all the memories he'd make at his new school. And maybe, his parents hoped, it would help him fit in. "No one's going to bully you here," his dad promised. "Your last school?

Those were bad kids. It's going to be different here. I got you something to help." It was a Polaroid camera—the old-fashioned kind. "We used to have these at parties," his dad explained. "Everybody loved them."

"How is this going to help me at school?" Harold asked. He loved his dad so much, and he appreciated what he was trying to do, but there was only so much his dad could do to help him fit in at school.

"Two words: photography club," Perry said with a smile. "I know this has been a hard year. But give it a shot. I think you might be pleasantly surprised."

Harold's dad wasn't wrong. He quickly found his people in the photography club. A girl named Nora was nice enough to let him join, but it was another girl—Sarah—who truly welcomed him in. She worked with him in the darkroom, and there was something about her that made him feel safe. He felt like he could be himself around her, and he began to let his guard down.

Over time, they became friends. True friends, the kind of friendship Harold had always wished he could have. One night, Sarah invited him to a party with all her friends.

"It's Eliza's birthday tomorrow," she told him. "We're having a party for her at Ben's house. You should come."

"Oh," Harold said, studying his film so he wouldn't have to look at her. "No thanks."

"Why won't you come?" Sarah asked, nudging him.

"Your friends are . . . cool," Harold said, finally glancing at her.

"You're cool," Sarah said without laughing. He could tell she meant it.

"No," he replied and laughed. "I'm definitely not cool. Ben's the quarterback. Victoria is going to be valedictorian. Eliza is a cheerleader. And Nora . . . she scares me."

"Never tell her that," Sarah said with a laugh. "She would die of satisfaction." She paused for a second, studying him in the blue light of the darkroom. "What happened at your last school that made you so scared of people?"

"It was . . . nothing."

"Just come, Harold," she urged. "It's just a party. And I can tell you some stuff about my friends that is super not cool."

But Harold didn't go. It was too much. Instead, he hid out in his basement workshop, sketching in his scrapbook.

He couldn't help being mad at himself. Why couldn't he just muster up the courage to go? Why couldn't he be like all the other kids?

Suddenly, he tossed his pencil aside and threw his chair at the wall. It felt good to let out some of his frustration. When the chair hit the wall, a brick knocked loose.

Harold suddenly heard something from within the basement wall. It was a voice. He stepped toward the wall and began removing bricks, one by one, until there was a hole large enough that he could reach inside the wall.

And that's when he found it: Slappy's case, right where Ephraim had left it nearly seventy years before.

Harold quickly grew obsessed with the dummy. He began bringing it every-where, despite his parents' protests. They knew it wasn't going to help Harold fit in; who brings a ventriloquist dummy to high school, for crying out loud?

But despite what his parents thought, Slappy did help Harold find his place at school. After Harold read the incantation on a card in the dummy's coat pocket one day, Slappy had come to life. And he helped Harold find his place. When Harold had the dummy, people admired him, found him funny, and accepted him.

Harold became part of Sarah's crowd and was soon eating lunch with Ben, Nora, Victoria, Eliza, and Sarah. Finally, finally, Harold had found his place. But Slappy didn't like to share, and he thought Sarah and her friends were a distraction from his greater goal.

One day, while Harold and Slappy were having a heated discussion after school, Nora stepped into the classroom and caught the two of them chatting. Nora's mouth dropped open when she realized what she was see-ing: Harold's dummy was talking. On its own. As if it were . . . alive, or something.

She raced through the halls to find Sarah. "There's something about that doll," she told her friend. "Something evil. I can't explain it."

As days passed, Harold grew more and more obsessed with Slappy. He knew the dummy was the only thing keeping him afloat—the only thing helping him fit in. But his parents disagreed. "Your father and I discussed it," Harold's mom said one morning when he came downstairs to leave for school, Slappy's case held tight like a life preserver in his hand. "And we don't think you should take the doll to school anymore."

"I have to take him to school," Harold protested. "I need him."

"Maybe you should be spending more time with your new, real friends and less time with, you know, a dummy."

"They weren't my real friends until Slappy," Harold pointed out. "I understand that now."

"Your friends will still be there without the doll—" Georgia began.

"Slappy," Harold snapped. "His name is Slappy, you toothless hag."

"What has gotten into you?" Perry cried out. "Do not speak to your mother that way." He snatched Slappy's case out of Harold's hand.

"I hate you," Harold said, looking from his mother to his father. Slappy had told him his parents were trying to ruin his life; they hated him, and they didn't care about his happiness. Harold snarled, "He's right. He's right about everything."

As soon as Harold was gone, Georgia grabbed the case. "I know this is dramatic," she said as she tossed Slappy into the fireplace, "but this thing creeps me out. I could have been imagining things, but I swear I saw it blink. Harold has been different ever since he found him." She glanced up at Harold's dad as she tossed a match into the fireplace and watched the fire roar to life. "He's going to hate us."

"I'll say it was an accident," Perry said with a shrug.

But Slappy couldn't be destroyed that easily. Despite the fire raging in the fireplace around him, the dummy wouldn't burn. When Harold returned home, coming back to get Slappy a few minutes after he left, he reeled on his parents. "You're killing him!" he screamed. "He's magic!"

Suddenly, Harold heard his best friend's voice calling to him from inside the fireplace. "It's time, Harold. Use the spell."

Anger flashed in Harold's eyes. The furniture began to shake. A vase fell off the mantle, and a light crashed to the floor. "What's going on?" Georgia asked, panicked.

"Harold?" Perry pleaded.

Harold was focused on one thing, and one thing alone: saving his best friend. "Adanna Meenu Sanara Kudarash." *Suddenly, his parents stilled. Their faces began to morph as they, too, turned into dummies.*

They had been Slappified.

Bye-bye, Biddle parents.

Over the following weeks, Harold and Slappy became more connected than ever. But Harold's friends could sense the change in him, and they were worried about how their friend was acting the more time he spent with Slappy.

"It's the puppet," Nora said while they were all talking about Harold one day. "I'm telling you guys, we're all in danger. We have to get it away from Harold."

"Everything changed when he found that dummy," Sarah said. "He told me he was scared."

"Yes," Nora said. "Because it's evil."

Ben shook his head. "I don't know about any evil dolls scaring people, but I do know it will drive Harold nuts. So, let's do it."

"Yeah," Eliza agreed. "Let's get that dummy."

"Tomorrow night." Ben nodded.

The next night, Harold's friends put their plan in motion. They were going to sneak into Harold's house and steal the dummy.

First, they rang the doorbell to distract him so they could slip in through the side door.

While Harold was out on the front porch, trying to figure out who'd rung the bell, Ben slipped into the basement. He grabbed Slappy off the table where he was sitting and shoved him into his case.

"Good-bye, you little idiot," Slappy said, his head swiveling to face Ben.

Ben dropped the doll in shock. He couldn't believe what he'd just seen. Had the dummy actually talked? "What the hell?" Ben gasped. Suddenly, an object flew across the room. Then the basement began to shake and the walls in the room began to crumble. Upstairs, a chandelier crashed to the floor right next to Harold. "Who's there?" Harold screamed from the living room.

The lights throughout the house flickered. Books began to pour off the built-in shelves. And then the house went dark. In the blackness, Ben managed to shove Slappy into his case and slammed it shut. Then he raced out of the basement, holding Slappy's case tight in his arms. He dashed through the living room, and a second later he heard Harold flick a match to light a candle. Then Harold hustled toward the basement door.

In the dining room, Ben met up with the others. "What happened down there?" Nora asked in a whisper.

"It was Slappy," Ben said, his voice hushed. He was freaking out; he didn't know how to process what he'd just seen.

The cuckoo clock began to chirp on repeat. Over and over, the clock droned—cuckoo, cuckoo, cuckoo. Harold slammed the door to the basement, locking himself in.

Ben ran toward the basement door. He pounded on it, screaming, "Harold, come out!"

From the other side of the basement door, Harold gasped and screamed, "Stay away from me!"

Suddenly, the house was alive with noises—their footsteps, slamming cabinets, the awful cuckoo clock on its endless loop.

"Open the door!" Nora demanded.

"Harold!" Sarah screamed, pounding again.

Suddenly, they heard a thud, followed by a crash. Moments later, smoke began to pour out from under the basement door. "Harold!" Sarah screamed again and again.

Rushing outside with the others to escape the smoke, Sarah screamed, "We have to get him out!" She charged back toward the house.

Suddenly, flames spit out the basement window, shattering the glass. For a moment, the flames formed the face of Harold Biddle. But only Nora could see the outline, and she knew immediately what it meant. "He's gone," she told the others. "Harold's gone."

"No," Sarah sobbed. "This isn't real."

"I told you it was," Nora snapped at her. "You didn't believe me."

"Now what?" Victoria asked. "Do we call someone?"

"No," Eliza told the others. "Harold's dead. Doesn't mean we have to ruin our lives, too. I can't go to jail. Grab the case."

Ben grabbed the case, and the five teens fled. But a few feet down the driveway, the case began to shake and move like there was something very alive inside. Ben set it down and it moved on its own. They all jumped back.

Sarah's hand flew to her mouth as the case popped open and Slappy sat up, staring at them. "Did you think it was going to be that easy?" Slappy scoffed.

Sarah screamed again as Ben grabbed Slappy, tearing the doll apart and stomping on it.

"Let's throw it in the fire," Eliza suggested.

"It won't burn," Nora told her. She had a sixth sense about these kinds of things. "We have to hide it where no one will ever look. My family's cabin. In the mountains—"

"No," Eliza argued. "Let's bury it in my dad's old mine. It's closed down. Nobody will ever find it."

"Then we can never, ever talk about what happened tonight again. Okay?" Ben looked around at the rest of the group. "Okay?"

They nodded in turn. But Sarah was the last. She couldn't stop staring at the burning Biddle house. Her friend Harold was gone.

NIGHT
OF THE
LIVING DUMMY

CHAPTER THIRTY-EIGHT

"Our parents went to get the puppet," Margot said after Nathan had finished telling them the stories of Ephraim Bratt and Harold Biddle. "Because it was evil."

"I don't know about you guys, but I'm super relieved," James said, flopping back into the couch in Nathan's living room.

"Okay," Lucas said, nodding. "So, good, our parents weren't real murderers."

Nathan gaped at them. "Um . . . yes, they were real murderers! That's what this story was all about. *Your parents* are the evil ones."

"Which is why Harold's ghost is trying to get back at them by haunting us," Isabella guessed. "Forcing me to almost kill my brother, getting Lucas to risk his life listening to worms, leaving James for dead?"

Nathan looked relieved. "You get it!"

"But," Lucas cut in, "it seems like Harold was kind of messed up, and our parents tried to help him."

"Listen to me," Nathan said, growing frustrated. "Your parents bullied Harold. Broke into his house. Stole his best friend—"

"Best friend?" James asked. A *puppet*?

Nathan ignored him and continued on, "And ended up killing him in the process. Were you guys not listening? That's the whole reason I told you this story!"

The five friends exchanged a look. Something about this guy was *off*. Finally, Margot spoke to break the tension that had settled in the room. "And how," she began, "do you know all this, Mr. Bratt?"

"Right," Nathan said, standing up. "The twist. I happen to know all this because I'm not Mr. Bratt. And it's time to get Slappy back." He held up the open scrapbook, and they saw what he'd been doodling inside the pages the whole time: the five of them, sitting on the couch in the living room at the Biddle house. As he showed them the newest addition to his scrapbook pages, flames engulfed his body. In the next moment, Nathan turned into the charred remains of Harold Biddle.

Lucas was closest to the door; he tugged on it. They had to get *out*. This Bratt—Biddle?—guy was *messed up*. But the door wouldn't budge. It appeared they were going nowhere fast.

"Mr. Bratt's gone," James announced suddenly, looking around the room. Where, just seconds before, a charred ghost of a person had stood, now there was nothing. No one.

"You mean Harold's gone," Margot pointed out.

"Where did he go?" James asked.

Lucas continued to tug at the door. "This is jammed, but I think I can get it." Reluctantly, Isaiah moved to help him. He wasn't eager to be friends with this dude who seemed to have stolen his girl (okay, to be totally honest, Margot didn't actually *know* she could be his girl yet, but *still*), but they had to get out of here somehow. Otherwise, he and Lucas would be trapped in this weird house together for even longer. And when you're being haunted by a dead kid and his creepy doll, beggars can't be choosers.

Isaiah stood behind Lucas, and on the count of three, they pushed the door open. But on the other side of the door was *not* the front porch. Instead, it was just open, terrifying blackness. A void where the outside world used to be.

Lucas and Isaiah realized this too late, and they both almost fell into the empty space on the other side of the door. Thankfully, Margot grabbed their arms and dragged them back into the living room while James slammed the door closed again. Wide-eyed, he stared at the others and said, "I'm going to vote for not opening things anymore."

Margot paced the living room while Isaiah went to try the basement door. It was locked. Margot suddenly realized something. "We're trapped in the scrapbook," she said. "Biddle must have drawn that picture of us in the scrapbook, to trap us here."

"I'm too young to die," James wailed.

"We're all the same age," Lucas noted drily.

"My mom will realize I'm gone and start freaking out soon enough," Isabella said.

"Yeah." James nodded, for once comforted by the fact that his mom seemed to *always* be keeping tabs on his whereabouts.

Isaiah added, "We've been gone all night. I'm sure they'll be here any minute now."

What they didn't know was that Biddle-Bratt had considered

that—and he'd taken care of things on his end to make sure *none* of the parents would come looking. He'd sent each parent a text from their child's phone, giving them all a believable story about why they would be late and why they shouldn't worry. The last thing he needed were his old "friends" turning up to "help" again.

After hours of waiting for someone to come and rescue them, the five friends were beginning to feel hopeless. "Has anyone considered the possibility that our parents won't be able to save us?" Margot said. "We need to do something other than just wait around and watch TV."

"Like what?" James asked.

"I don't know," Margot said. "Explore whatever this is."

James shook his head quickly. "Your 'exploring' is what got us into this mess in the first place."

"Um, *this* is not my fault," Margot argued.

"I'm just saying," James began, "if it had to be someone's fault, my vote is for you. We came in to get you, and now I'm trapped in a scrapbook after being trapped in a mine after being trapped in a house by a cuckoo clock!"

"If you're looking to blame someone," Isaiah said, trying to get his friend to chill and defend his—Margot, "it's our parents who caused this ghost to seek revenge on us for *their* sins, not Margot's."

"Thank you," Margot said, offering him a grateful smile.

Isaiah added, "But we did tell you not to go into the haunted scrapbook."

Suddenly, Isabella held up a hand. "Wait. Do you guys hear that?" She clicked off the TV, and everyone listened to the overwhelming silence. Suddenly, there was a very audible creaking coming from somewhere else in the house.

"It's coming from the dining room," Margot whispered.

"We should hide," Isabella said.

"Hide where?" James hissed back. "It's just one big room!"

"I'm sick of hiding," Isaiah said. He grabbed a candlestick off a table, then began a slow creep toward the dining room. The others each grabbed a random weapon of their own and followed him. As they rounded the corner, Isaiah whispered, "One . . . two . . . three!"

They all charged. "It's him!" Isaiah screamed as the group came face-to-face with Nathan. "It's Harold Biddle!"

All five of them raised their weapons to charge, but Nathan waved his hands in the air. "Stop! No! No, no, no! I'm not Harold Biddle. I'm me. Nathan Bratt. The *real* Nathan Bratt. Your English teacher. I was possessed by a ghost or something."

The group slowly lowered their weapons, looking at one another to see who believed this. It felt crazy, but what *didn't* seem crazy these past few weeks?

Isabella continued to hold her weapon at the ready, just in case this was all a trick. She said, "I'm going to need a little more information before I put this fire poker down."

CHAPTER
THIRTY-NINE

Back at the hospital, Nora had taken Sarah's advice and stopped taking the pills Victoria had been issuing her. Now, finally, she had clarity. Sarah was right; she had to stop talking about Harold if she had any hope of getting out. "I think I'm starting to see things more clearly now," Nora told Victoria. "I'm a lot less fuzzy and sleepy all the time. Know anything about that?"

Victoria shrugged. "I did my best."

"You drugged me," Nora said, making sure her old friend knew exactly what Nora had figured out.

"Nora, let's not get carried away," Victoria said.

"How about let's *do* get carried away, Victoria," Nora snapped. "There is a ghost coming after our children." Then she spun on her heel and checked herself out of the hospital. It was time to deal with this, once and for all. No more pretending what happened that night didn't happen; ignoring Harold wasn't going to make him forget and go away.

In the elevator, Nora bumped into the new high school English teacher. Mr. Bratt, was it? "Oh . . . hi," she said, confused about what he was doing there.

"Just the person I was looking for," Nathan said.

Nora frowned. "Why were you looking for me?"

"You know," Nathan said, grinning like a lunatic. "Our mutual friend."

"What mutual friend?" Nora said. She'd been feeling clear again, but now she was just as confused as she had been when she was taking Victoria's prescribed meds. "What are you talking about?"

Suddenly, Nora noticed her reflection in the elevator doors. And there, standing beside her, was not Nathan Bratt, but Harold Biddle. He waved at her. "Harold . . ." Nora breathed.

She turned to him, and he lunged at her. "I want him back," Biddle-Bratt growled. "I know you went to the mine and took him out of that case." Nora looked down and saw that Biddle-Bratt was holding Slappy's eyeball in his hand.

He had found the eye where Lucas had lost it outside the saw-mill, after all that business with the worms. He had a *piece* of his best friend back. Now he wanted the rest of him. "Give him back to me."

The elevator doors slid open then, and Nora took her chance. She dashed out of the elevator and ran. She knew exactly where Slappy was, and she had to get to him before Biddle did. As soon as she got home, she flew into the old shed. She grabbed the duffle bag where Slappy's broken body had been stuffed since she'd pulled the dummy out of the mine. A tiny doll hand was sticking out of the top. Suddenly, Nora heard a sound behind her, so she hastily shoved the bag back onto the shelf. Spinning around, she found Colin standing there.

"Nora?" he said. "I was coming by to get your mail and water the plants. But . . . you got discharged? Without calling me?" Colin had been eager to talk to Nora. He needed to tell her that he'd had a talk with Sarah, and things between them were officially over. Their separation was now permanent; Sarah wouldn't be coming home. He and Nora could be together for real, without all the secrets.

"I'm sorry. It happened really fast," Nora said, distracted. "There's something I need to do right away, before I can see anyone."

"Even Lucas?" Colin asked. He knew how close Nora was to her son, and he was surprised she wasn't eager to see him now that she was out. He stepped aside as Nora grabbed a duffel bag off the shelf behind her, looking like she was trying to get past him. "Okay, well . . . what exactly is it that you're doing in here?"

"I'm just taking care of something," she said. "It won't take long." She raced away, leaving Colin reeling and confused. Nora tossed the bag with Slappy's remains into the back of her car and drove quickly through and out of town. She got on the highway, heading for the one place she could think of to hide Slappy. She knew the old puppet was indestructible. The only option was to hide him where no one would ever find him again.

As soon as Nora had driven away, Colin headed for Ben's house. He needed to know why Nora was acting so weird, and her old friend Ben might have some clues for him. He really wanted to get this thing with Nora to work, but he was at a loss for how to get her to open up. As a guidance counselor, he knew his best bet was to talk it out. "Hey, Colin," Ben said, swinging the door open. "What's up?"

"I could really use someone to talk to about relationship stuff . . ."

Ben waved him inside and offered him a seat in the kitchen. "So, this is about Sarah?"

Colin shook his head. "Nora."

"Oh," Ben said, shocked. "*Oh*."

"Yeah," Colin said quickly. Sarah had found out about him and Nora, and truth be told, it was about time. She'd abandoned him and Margot long ago, and she couldn't expect him to wait around for her to change her mind and come back to them. "Sarah knows. It's out in the open. So, I just stopped by because I know you and Nora go way back."

"Is she doing okay after, you know . . . ?" Ben asked. He was worried about Nora. She'd always had a sixth sense about stuff, and everything with Harold resurfacing after all this time was making him a little nervous.

"I thought so," Colin said with a sigh. "But she was acting pretty weird just now. Like, not her normal weird."

"Can you be more specific?" Ben prompted.

"She wouldn't talk to me. Is there something I don't know about Nora? Some sort of repressed memory that was unlocked recently? Did you guys run over a doll or something in high school?" He laughed at this ridiculous suggestion.

But Ben gaped at him. "What did you just say?"

"Yeah," Colin said, still chuckling about what he'd seen Nora carrying out of the shed. "She had, like, doll parts stuffed in a duffel bag that she had in her shed . . ."

Ben jumped up and grabbed his car keys. "Where is Nora? Where is she now?"

"I don't know," Colin said. "She took off. She didn't tell me where she was going—"

Before Colin could finish what he was saying, Ben ran out of the house, got in his truck, and zoomed away. Colin stared after him, the second person to ditch him in a hurry in less than an hour. "I'm starting to feel like it's me . . ."

CHAPTER FORTY

"I can't believe nobody noticed you were possessed by a ghost," Isaiah said after Nathan had told them the story of how his body had been taken over by Harold Biddle. "I feel like my parents or whoever I was dating or my best friend . . . someone would have definitely noticed."

Nathan explained, "I'm in a transitional period of life."

Margot looked worried. "And you've been here for how long?"

"Since the night of his game," Nathan said, glancing at Isaiah.

"That was a long time ago," James mused, suddenly realizing that they could be stuck here for way longer than any of them had considered.

Isaiah heard this, but he wasn't willing to accept Nathan's same fate. "Okay, if there was a way in, there has to be a way out."

"I agree with Isaiah," Isabella said. She'd been poking around, looking for an exit. "And I think I see something." She'd scrambled on her belly to look down into the open chasm outside the front door. "There's a light down there. Do you see it?"

Way down below them, there was a light. And something dim that appeared to be floating in the darkness. "Oh my god," Nathan said, his voice registering shock. "Another floating room!"

"You've been here for a minute, and you've never looked out

the door?" James asked. The dude had just accepted his fate, and had done *nothing* to try to help himself? Yeesh.

"Here's the thing," Nathan explained. "I saw the abyss and never looked at it again, because—it's terrifying."

"I can get down there," Isabella said, hopping to her feet. She started pulling drapes down from the windows and began tying them together, fashioning a sort of rope. The others could see what she was working on, and everyone joined in to help her.

But once the rope was ready, Isaiah suddenly had a flash of panic. "I don't think you should go. You're volunteering to go down into a gigantic black abyss, which seems insane."

"That's why I want to go," Isabella said. "I mean, when have I ever had a chance to do something like this?"

"But Lucas does stupid stuff like this all the time," Isaiah told her. He figured this was a perfect chance to offload the spare. "Maybe he should go."

"Yes, I am the expert on stupid stuff," Lucas said, glaring back at Isaiah. Then he nodded at Isabella and said, "And I think she's got this."

"Me too," Margot agreed.

"Okay, fine!" Isaiah snapped. "Everyone jump all over me for being concerned for our friend."

James held up his hands, innocently. "Hey, bro. I didn't pile on while everyone else was piling. That's, like, partial solidarity."

"Okay," Nathan said, breaking in. "So, are you going to try to save me, or what?"

"Let's do this," Isabella said, moving toward the gaping

doorway. She held the makeshift rope in her hands, ready to be lowered down into the abyss. It was time to see what was in the other room that was floating below them.

"How are you going to communicate?" James asked her.

"One pull every minute means I'm good," Isabella said. "And two quick pulls means you gotta yank me up." She caught Isaiah's eyes. He still looked worried. Isabella felt a warm feeling in her chest that almost made her forget about the dangerous, truly insane thing she was about to do. "I'll be fine. I promise."

Slowly, carefully, they began to lower Isabella down. She passed through what felt like miles of blackness before finally, her feet touched solid ground below. She looked around. It was a hallway with lockers. PLHS, but from years ago. Suddenly, she heard laughter coming from a doorway just down the hall. She stepped through it, walking out onto the stage in the school auditorium. Onstage, there was a spotlight, but no performer.

Isabella stepped into the circle of light, then turned to the audience. What she saw froze her in place. Every person in the audience looked like a ventriloquist dummy. But they weren't like Slappy. Their features and clothes were all too realistic looking. With a flash, Isabella realized this wasn't a room of Slappy's fellow puppets. These had been *real* people—all victims of the dangerous doll. And based on the various styles of dress the dummies were in, he had been at this for a lot longer than any of them realized.

Isabella spun around and ran back in the direction she'd come, eager to get out of the nightmare she'd dropped into.

Meanwhile, out in the real world, Biddle-Bratt had his sights set on Nora, who was driving quickly out of town. Suddenly, he spit the gum in his mouth into his hand. Searching for something to put it in, Biddle-Bratt saw the scrapbook sitting open on the seat beside him. He glanced at it, noticing a picture of Sarah staring up at him from a page decorated to look like the school hallway.

"Sorry, Sarah," Biddle-Bratt said, tearing the page out of the scrapbook to stuff his gum inside. He tossed the ripped-out sheet of paper onto the floor of the car and continued on his merry way, in hot pursuit of Nora and his best friend, Slappy.

Suddenly, the hallway began to shake. Isabella yanked on the curtain rope twice, hoping her friends would tug her up—now. Something was happening. The world of the scrapbook around her was crumbling, disappearing, falling apart.

"She yanked twice!" Isaiah cried from up above. "She yanked twice!"

The group began to pull her up, desperately scrabbling at the curtain rope to try to get their friend out of there.

The rope was harder to control bringing her up than it was when they lowered her down. It slipped through their fingers, but everyone grabbed on tightly as, all of a sudden, the rope snapped them all forward.

Trying to hold things steady in his spot at the back of the rope, the force slammed Nathan against a wall—and he *disappeared*! But in their focus to bring Isabella up, no one else realized he was gone.

Suddenly, Nathan was back in his body—his real body—inside the car with the scrapbook. He couldn't believe it! Had the force of hitting the wall knocked him back into the real world somehow? But when he glanced in the rearview mirror, he saw Harold's face looking straight back at him.

In the next moment, Nathan was back in the world of the scrapbook again. Isabella was up out of the abyss, back in the Biddle living room, and so was he.

"What happened down there?" James was asking her.

"It seemed like the past," Isabella said, panting. "But it felt like the future. I can't explain it. And everyone I saw looked like a puppet."

James groaned. "This day keeps getting better and better."

Nathan blurted, "I think I have a way out. But I'm not totally sure yet." He turned to Isaiah and said, "Hit me."

"Hit you?" Isaiah asked, confused.

Nathan suddenly realized he'd picked the wrong person to hit him. He looked at James and said, "Actually, *you* hit me."

James reeled back. "No."

A second later, Isabella stepped forward and slapped Nathan. The same thing happened as when he'd hit the wall—for one split second, he was back in his body, driving the car. But then, moments later, he'd already been whooshed back to his spot inside the scrapbook world. "I was right!" he cried, turning to the kids. "I was back in my body. Pain seems to make me go back into my *real* body!"

"Are you serious?" James asked.

"I was in my car," Nathan told them. "And the scrapbook was there, too. On the seat next to me."

"That's it!" Margot said, snapping. "That's how we're getting home. If Mr. Bratt can get to the scrapbook, he can write us out of here!"

Nathan smirked. "I am a bit of a writer, not to brag. I've had a few stories and a want ad published in *Horror Weekly*."

"You need to add an exit," Margot told him. "A way out, to the page that we're on right now."

Lucas realized what this meant. "We have to send him back." They all spun around, ready to knock Nathan back into his real body.

Isabella was the one to strike the blow again. But this time, she nailed him harder, hoping maybe that would keep him in his body longer, and give him enough time to find out what Biddle-Bratt was up to, so Nathan could write them out of this nightmare.

Reeling from the impact, Nathan snapped into his real body just in time to see Nora walking away from her car into a general store across the street. He was parked nearby, the scrapbook safely beside him in the passenger seat. He began to roll down the window, but his hand stopped against his will. He looked into the mirror and saw the ghost of Harold Biddle staring back at him.

Whoosh!

"What happened?" James asked as soon as Nathan was back inside the scrapbook world.

"Biddle pushed me back out," Nathan explained. "But I saw Nora."

"My mom?" Lucas asked.

Nathan nodded. "Outside an old general store in the mountains."

"I know that store!" Lucas said. "That's near our cabin. What's she doing up there?"

"I don't know," Nathan said. "But Biddle must be following her."

"Did you see the scrapbook?" Margot asked.

"Yes, it's on the passenger seat."

"You've got to get us out of here!" Lucas cried. If Harold was after his mom, he had to get there. He had to help her! Lucas wound up, and before Nathan could protest, he knocked his fist into his teacher's face, sending him back into the real world.

As soon as he was in his body inside the parked car, Nathan reached for the scrapbook. But Harold still had partial control, and he wasn't about to let Nathan ruin this for him. He and Nathan were at war, both acting out a different plan within the same body. As they fought for control over their shared human form, Nathan suddenly gained enough power to grab the scrapbook and fling it across the car.

With Harold powering the right side of his body, Nathan didn't have a lot of options for what to do with it. He lobbed the scrapbook out the open window, with a plan to get out of the car and hopefully away from the ghost of Harold Biddle altogether. But instead, the scrapbook landed in a puddle of water. It was open to the page that had first trapped the teens in the scrapbook. The five friends were sketched on the page, right inside the living room of the Biddle house. As Nathan watched through the car window, he could see the ink begin to fade and run, disintegrating the page and the scene altogether.

"What's going on?" Isabella asked, noticing that the walls around them were dripping—as if they were made of wet ink.

Suddenly, they dropped, landing in a different scene. With a scream, they looked around to try to figure out what was going on. But before they could, they dropped again, into Harold Biddle's basement.

A hand reached out of the darkness and clutched Margot's shoulder. She screamed, turning to see two ghosts—a man and a woman—emerging from the shadows.

"Don't be scared," the woman said.

The man added, "We're Harold's parents."

"Great," James said. This whole thing was getting weirder and weirder. "Your son is holding us hostage so he can get Slappy back."

"You can't let that happen," Harold's mom told them.

"What are we supposed to do?" Isabella asked. "We're trapped in here like you."

"No," Harold's mom said. "We're not trapped. We're waiting for him so we can move on together."

Just then, outside the general store, Nathan gained enough control over his body to get out of the car. He grabbed the scrapbook from the puddle, flipping through the wet pages quickly, noticing the ink on so many of them had faded and run. He finally peeled the first page of the scrapbook back and noticed that the ink from the sketch of the five kids in the living room had been transferred onto the Biddle basement page of the scrapbook. Hoping he knew what this meant, Nathan grabbed a pen and began to draw a door . . .

"That's it!" Margot said, turning away from Harold's parents to point at a bright line that had suddenly appeared inside the basement where they were standing. "Mr. Bratt did it! He drew a door, and that's our way out. Everyone go!"

Just as she was about to step through with the others, Harold's dad pulled Margot back and said, "Tell him we forgive him. And that he'll always be our Harebear."

The basement continued to drip, fading away to almost nothing just before Margot stepped through the crudely drawn portal. She landed inside the Biddle house, back in the living room again.

But this time, it was the real world. They'd done it, they'd escaped the scrapbook.

"We have to find my mom," Lucas said, rushing to the door.

Nathan maintained control of his own body just long enough to see the five teens disappear from the basement page of the scrapbook. It seemed he'd done it; they'd made it safely out. But then Harold took over his body once again, snapping Nathan back into the lonely world of the scrapbook, leaving Harold in complete control over Nathan's physical body once more.

CHAPTER FORTY-ONE

"We promised we'd never come back," Eliza said, sitting inside her car with Ben later that day. They were parked outside the old mine, the place she'd come to with the others so many years before to hide Slappy—and hadn't stepped foot in since.

Ben took the keys to the mine from her, and said, "Well, it seems one of us broke that promise." He stepped out of the car and said, "Wait here."

Inside the mine, Ben poked through the darkness, searching for the old mine shaft where they'd hidden Slappy. He'd never forget the last place he'd seen that awful doll. But when he got to the spot he was looking for, he found a hole with dirt piled up next to it.

"It's not there," said a male voice from somewhere above him. Ben jumped back, shining his flashlight up to the upper edge of the pit.

"James?" Ben said, confused. "What are you doing here? Did your mom tell you about this?"

The Dupe James smirked down at him. "She's not my mom," he said. "But I'm going to deal with her as soon as I'm done with you." He kicked at Ben's ladder, leaving him stuck at the bottom of the pit.

Moments later, outside the mine, Eliza watched the door of the mine eagerly. When she saw the door open, she let herself relax.

Thank god, Ben was back. But it wasn't Ben; it was . . . her son? "James!" she said, jumping out of her SUV. "Oh my god, look at you! Is this where you spent the night with your friends? Did you turn the family mine into a drug den?"

Dupe James chortled out a strange laugh. "I think someone is projecting," he said, cocking his head. "I'm definitely not the one with the problem here, Eliza. It's time for you to start living the truth. You have to pay for what you did to Harold."

The blood drained from her face. Dupe James swept a loose board off the ground and came at her, menacingly. "You're not James," she said, suddenly realizing. What Nora had been telling them was right. Something strange was going on, and it all had to do with Harold.

"Nope," Dupe James said, grinning. Just as he raised the board above his head, ready to crack it over Eliza's skull, something crashed into him from behind. Ben wrestled the board out of Dupe James's hands. But the dupe was surprisingly strong, and even though Ben was a former football player, he was having a hard time gaining the upper hand. Just as Dupe James wrapped his arms around Ben, trying to choke the life out of him, Eliza scrambled to pick up the board. She swung it through the air, and the duplicate exploded into a messy splat of goop.

"Well," Eliza said as she looked down at Ben, who was now covered in sticky green goo, "I think it's safe to say Nora's been right all along."

Nora drove up a snowy mountain road quickly, grateful for the chains on her tires. There was a storm coming, and the mountains could be very dangerous in this kind of weather. But it was worth the risk to get rid of Slappy, to bury him somewhere no one would ever find that awful dummy again.

She stopped at the top of the mountain, right outside a small cabin. She headed inside with the supplies she'd purchased at the general store and the duffel bag that contained what was left of Slappy.

Just as she was gathering up her shovel, someone appeared outside the cabin door. Nora jumped. But when she saw it was a park ranger, her nerves settled. That dummy had her on high alert.

She swung open the door and the ranger said, "I'm just swinging by cabins up here and making sure everyone knows a storm is coming in fast, and it's going to be a bad one. Could be a six-foot dump."

"I'm not going to be here very long," Nora told him.

"Well, I'll get going. Got a few more cabins to swing by before we close down the road coming up here."

As soon as the ranger was gone, Nora closed the door behind him and walked to the window to watch him drive away. She let out a sigh of relief, but then a voice behind her said, "I thought he would never leave."

Slappy.

Nora glared at the bag and that puppet—that awful puppet. She ran across the room and began shoving pieces of the dummy back into the duffel bag. "I can help you," Slappy told her, his head the only thing sticking out of the bag.

"I don't understand how you're talking right now," Nora said. The dummy was broken, split into pieces. Nothing about this made any sense.

"You've always been special, Nora," Slappy crooned. "I want to help you. Put me back together."

Nora glared back at the dummy. "You're not going to 'help' anyone else ever again," she vowed. "I'm going to hide you in these mountains, where nobody will ever find you." Then she wrapped thick duct tape around Slappy's mouth, trying to silence him—for good.

"You can't stop me!" Slappy argued, his voice muffled through the tape.

With one mighty shove, Nora pressed his head down inside the duffel bag and cinched it closed. Then she stepped out into the snow and began her quest to end this nightmare for good.

CHAPTER FORTY-TWO

Nathan's car was poorly equipped for the mountain roads. As he drove up the mountain after Nora, Biddle-Bratt was struggling to maintain control of his car on the slippery pass. Suddenly, a park ranger stepped out in front of his car and held up a hand for him to stop.

"Where are you headed?" the ranger asked.

"I was following a friend," Biddle-Bratt explained, "but I lost her. Blond hair, station wagon."

"Oh, yeah!" the park ranger said, his face brightening. "I just saw her. She has that cabin on Timberlane Drive. You just head up this road right here and turn left at the first fork. You can't miss it."

Biddle-Bratt grinned. "Thank you."

"But you can't go," the ranger told him. "The road is already a mess up there. You have to have chains."

"I don't have *time* for chains," Biddle-Bratt growled. He threw the car in reverse and began to drive back down the mountain. But before he went far, he pulled the car to the side of the road. He parked and headed up the mountain on foot, in the direction the park ranger had pointed, making his way through the snow straight toward Nora's cabin.

A little farther down the mountain, Lucas was fretting inside the backseat of James's Jeep. "What if we're too late?" he asked the others as James made the slow, treacherous drive up the mountain toward the Parker family's old cabin.

"Don't worry," James tried to assure him. "We're not too late. Mr. Bratt slowed him way down."

"I hope you're right," Lucas murmured.

James glanced at his worried friend in the rearview mirror. Pressing his foot down harder on the pedal, he said, "Permission to drive like I promised my mother I never would?" Then he floored it.

Not much farther up the road, Lucas sat up straight and yelled, "Wait! Stop."

James slammed on the brakes.

Lucas pointed to a car on the side of the road. "That's Mr. Bratt's car."

All five of them hopped out of the Jeep to investigate. Wind and snow whipped wildly around. Lucas headed toward the abandoned car, the others close on his heels. "Over here," James called out suddenly. He pointed. There were footprints heading away from the car, right up the edge of the mountain.

"Oh my god," Lucas said. "He's on foot. And he's headed straight for the cabin." He immediately began to march through the fresh snow to follow the prints.

"No, Lucas!" Margot called after him. She wasn't about to let her new boyfriend go after their possessed teacher in weather like this. "The storm. We have to wait."

"There's no time to wait. I have to get to my mom." Lucas began to run. He wasn't going to let anything keep him from protecting her. She was all that was left of his family, and he wasn't going to let Harold get to her.

"I'm not letting Lucas go up there alone," Margot said, charging after him.

Isaiah watched as Margot plunged into the snow and chased after Lucas. He didn't have to think about it; he was going, too. There was no way he was letting Margot and Lucas do this on their own. "Then I'm going with you, too," he called out.

"But what if Nathan comes back, with Nora?" Isabella asked. She didn't want Isaiah to go. She felt like they were finally getting closer, to the point where maybe, finally, they could be something together. But instead, he was leaving her to protect Margot. As always, Isabella was invisible. This time, even to the one person who had finally started to notice her in the way she had always craved.

"Good point," Isaiah said. He gestured to James and Isabella, not noticing Isabella's concern for him. "You guys stay here. Together. You'll be safer."

"We gotta go," Margot cried out through the wind and snow. She turned again, charging up the steep, snowy pass behind Lucas, with Isaiah right behind her.

"It's okay," James told Isabella, who looked like she was pissed she'd been left behind. "If staying here in my warm car with heated seats is what's needed from us in this moment, then we'll do it. We'll step up." James glanced at her as the others marched out of sight. He could tell this wasn't helping, so he decided to try another approach. Isabella thought no one could see how she felt about Isaiah, but James could. He could always tell when people were hiding something important. "You know Isaiah and Margot will never be together."

"What?" Isabella said.

"They're an *almost couple*. They can't actually be together, or the magic of 'them' will be gone. They're in love with the *idea* of each other, but they'd never make it work for real." Isabella looked at James doubtfully and he shrugged in response. "My point is that they never want to *actually* get there. You're fine."

Isabella blinked. "So let me get this right: I can date Isaiah as long as I'm okay with him having deep-seated, unresolved feelings for his beautiful neighbor?"

"Exactly!" James said, not noticing the very obvious devastated look on his friend's face. "Now that that's settled, are you hungry? I'm hungry. Do you think Postmates delivers up here?"

CHAPTER
FORTY-THREE

Nora pulled the duffel bag tight and slung it over her shoulder. But when she opened the door to the cabin, she stopped short. There was someone approaching in the distance. It was Nathan—no, Harold—and he was on foot. She raced quickly to her car, lugging the duffel bag behind her.

When she made it to her station wagon, the bag began to shake and move on the passenger seat. It was as though Slappy could sense the presence of Harold nearby, and it was slowly bringing him back to life.

Nora turned the key, but the engine wouldn't turn over. She tried and failed again and again to get the car to start. Suddenly, Biddle-Bratt slammed his hands down on the hood of her car. Nora stared at him through the windshield, and he glared back at her, fury painted across his face.

"We belong together," he shouted.

"He's evil," Nora screamed back. "He made *you* evil."

"He made me *special*!"

Nora shook her head. "No, he made you a monster."

"He didn't do this to me," Biddle-Bratt said, moving to the driver's side window. "You and your friends did."

Smash! He punched through the driver's side window, grabbing onto Nora's coat. Finally, Nora got the engine to start. It roared to life and she punched her foot down on the gas. The car jolted forward, dragging Biddle-Bratt along for a few feet before he finally let go of her coat and fell to the ground, clutching his leg.

For a second, Nora thought she was in the clear. But just a little farther up the road, her car got stuck in a ditch, and she knew it wasn't going any farther in this weather. With no other choice, she grabbed the duffel bag and got out of the car. She ran away on foot, diving deep into the snowy forest, while the injured Biddle-Bratt chased desperately after her.

But the snow—coupled with Biddle-Bratt's injury and Nora's heavy duffel bag—prevented either of them from moving too quickly. And the weather was getting worse by the minute. The snow was falling so thickly that Nora couldn't even see her pursuer behind her. But she could hear him, so she knew he was close.

"What's your plan, Nora?" he taunted, his voice carrying across the wind. "Toss him away like you tossed me down the basement steps? You can run as long as you want, but you won't get far. I don't care if we freeze to death out here; I'm already dead."

Lucas, Isaiah, and Margot finally reached the cabin, but it was immediately clear Nora wasn't there anymore. The door to the cabin was open, and there was no one inside. Then, Lucas noticed her car just down the road, stuck in a ditch, the drivers' side window smashed. "Mom!" Lucas cried, running to the car. But the car was empty.

Isaiah pointed at fresh prints, heading farther up the hill. "She ran toward the trees."

"It's gonna be okay," Margot said, trying to calm Lucas down. "We'll find her."

The snow was so intense now that they could only see about two feet in each direction. "Stay close," Isaiah instructed the others as they set off into the ever-deepening snow. "We don't want to get separated."

Back at the car, Isabella and James were getting worried. "They should have been back by now," Isabella said, staring off in the direction Isaiah had disappeared far too long ago.

"I know," James said. Moments later, a car honked behind them.

"James?" Eliza said, rolling down her window. The other parents were in the car with her.

"Isabella?" Victoria said, climbing out of the car. "What are you doing up here?"

"It's a long story," Isabella said. "What are you guys doing here?"

"It's also a long story," her mom answered.

Ben walked toward the other car parked along the side of the snowy road. "Is this Nathan Bratt's car? Where is Isaiah?"

James explained, "He went to Nora's cabin with Lucas and Margot."

Sarah looked panicked. "Margot's out there?"

"Which direction?" Ben asked. James pointed at the tracks, which were quickly being covered by the storm. Ben stepped into the snow. "Let's go."

Everyone followed as Ben marched up the mountain. James explained to the parents, "Nora headed up there with Slappy."

"You know about Slappy?" Sarah asked quickly.

"We know about everything," Isabella said. Then she added, "It's okay. I mean, it's not great. But I think we understand you guys a lot better now."

"Mom!" Nora heard her son's voice calling to her from somewhere up ahead. Lucas had come to help her! She spun around, desperately trying to see which direction her son was in. She'd lost Biddle-Bratt, but with the snow, she had no idea how close he might be. She knew she had to keep moving, but if she had backup, this would make everything a whole lot easier. Still, she didn't want Lucas mixed up in any of this. What was he *doing* out here?

"Lucas? I'm here!"

"Follow the sound of my voice!" Lucas called out.

"I hear you, sweetie," she said, rushing through the snow to get to him. "I'm coming."

"I'm this way. Mom, I think I can see you. Can you see me?"

She could make out a silhouette in the distance. He began to wave his hands in the air.

"I can see you!" she cried out. "I'm coming, Lucas!" Nora began to run toward him. But as she drew nearer, she got a clearer look at the figure. It wasn't her son; it was Biddle-Bratt.

"I thought I wouldn't find you," Biddle-Bratt said, still in Lucas's voice. "But you came right to me."

Nora screamed. She spun around and ran in the opposite direction. But Biddle-Bratt was close enough to grab the duffel off her shoulder. As he pulled it from her grasp, Nora lost her balance and plummeted down a steep embankment.

Biddle-Bratt clutched the duffel in his arms and glanced down. Nora was in a pile of snow at the bottom of the hill, clearly unconscious. "Now if you could just die there," Biddle-Bratt called out, "that would be great."

He poured the Slappy pieces out of the bag onto the snowy ground. Finally, *finally*, he had his best friend back. Quickly, he pulled the missing eyeball out of his pocket, and popped it back into Slappy's face. With a blink, Slappy turned to face Biddle-Bratt and said, "Hello, old friend."

CHAPTER FORTY-FOUR

Lucas, Isaiah, and Margot still hadn't found Nora. They were getting colder and more worried by the minute. As the snow intensified, Lucas picked up his pace, and Margot hustled to keep up with him. Isaiah was holding up the rear of the pack, but he had begun to fall farther and farther behind. He could just barely see Margot's back through the snow, and he scrambled to try to catch her. But then, suddenly, his foot slipped, and he slid off the edge of a cliff.

Amid the snow and wind, Lucas and Margot didn't hear him fall. They continued to trek through the woods, leaving Isaiah alone, dangling from the embankment.

Isaiah had managed to catch himself with his good arm and was hanging from the edge, but he wouldn't be able to hold himself there for long. He tried to pull himself up, but with one arm useless in its cast, he couldn't do it. He desperately called out, "Lucas? Margot?"

Nothing.

"Can you hear me?!" It was clear no one was coming for him.

Isaiah considered the situation and realized he had two possible options. He would have to figure out some way to climb up or he would fall down the mountain. And if the fall didn't kill him, the cold definitely would. Given the options, Isaiah knew his only choice was to drag himself up and out. It was time to dig deep. He braced himself against the edge of the cliff, using rocks as footholds. Slowly, carefully, he made his way up, straining with every pull and step, until finally he was back to the spot where he had first fallen.

He peeked up and over the edge of the embankment and found himself face-to-face with a creepy ventriloquist dummy. "Hello," Slappy said, that awful smile plastered on his carved, wooden face.

Isaiah freaked out, and his unconscious jerk away from the dummy caused him to slip, losing his tenuous foothold. He dangled by just his one good hand again. "Oops," Biddle-Bratt said, leaning over the edge to peer at him hanging there. "Did we scare you?"

Margot and Lucas had finally noticed their friend was no longer behind them. Now they had *two* people they were searching for in the snowy forest, and neither had any idea which way to go. "Isaiah?!" Lucas screamed.

"First your mom, now Isaiah," Margot said. "I'm really scared. What if—"

Just then, Margot slipped in the snow. Lucas grabbed her arm just before she slid out of sight. Lucas looked down, realizing just how bad it could have been if he hadn't caught her. The embankment was steep, the bottom far. But when he looked down to see just *how* far, he spotted his mom laying still at the bottom, partially covered in snow. "Mom!" he screamed.

"Oh my god," Margot said.

The two of them began to pick their way carefully down the steep hill to get to her. Just as Lucas reached her, Nora opened her eyes. When she saw Lucas towering over her, she muttered, "Am I dead?"

"I hope not," Lucas said, touching her face. "Because that means I am, too." Nora began to cry with relief. "There's no time to cry. We have to get out of here and find Harold."

"You know about Harold," Nora said, finally realizing why her son was out here. "I'm sorry. I never wanted this to affect you."

"Everything that affects you, affects me," Lucas told her. "If we make it out of this . . . no more secrets."

Nora nodded. "No more secrets."

They began to pick their way back up the embankment. Now that they had his mom, Lucas knew they had to find Isaiah next. Trekking back in the direction they'd come from, Lucas was starting to worry if they'd ever find him. And that's when he spotted Biddle-Bratt and Slappy, sitting atop the edge of a cliff. He could hear Biddle-Bratt saying, "This is actually a really nice moment, because the last person I saw before I died was your dad. So I'm, like, paying it forward."

Then Isaiah's voice cried out, "Wait! You got it all wrong!"

Lucas rushed forward. He grabbed Biddle-Bratt and pulled him away from the edge of the cliff, just as Biddle-Bratt was about to slam Isaiah's good hand with a rock.

Biddle-Bratt threw Lucas off him and spun around to face Nora and Margot.

"Harold, don't do this!" Nora called out, trying to get her old friend's attention. "This isn't who you are."

Slappy disagreed. "Harold, it is who you are."

Nora looked only at Biddle-Bratt when she said, "He ruined all our lives. You know that better than anyone."

Margot called out, "We talked to your parents!"

"My parents are dead!" Biddle-Bratt screamed back.

"So are you, Harold," Nora said.

Slappy sneered. "Thanks to them."

Isaiah was still holding on to the edge of the cliff for dear life. Biddle-Bratt glanced at Ben's son, then turned back to Nora and said, "You destroyed me, and now I'm going to destroy you."

Just then, James, Isabella, and the other parents stumbled into view in the snowy woods. "Oh my god," Victoria gasped, watching as Nathan's face began to change into Harold's. Slowly, Harold was completely overtaking Nathan's body. It was finally obvious to everyone what was going on.

"It's really him," Ben said, realizing. "It's Harold."

"You guys can see him now, too?" Nora asked, relieved.

Sarah stepped forward. "Harold, you were my friend. You were my brilliant friend. We were trying to save you, but we failed. In every way. You have to believe us."

"Don't listen to them," Slappy ordered.

"We saw your parents," Margot said again. "In the scrapbook. They're refusing to move on without you. They need you."

"And they forgive you," Lucas added.

"Just like we hope you'll forgive us," Ben said.

"You can't trust what they're saying," Slappy snapped. "Harold, finish them off. Just like you did your parents."

Biddle-Bratt stepped backward toward the edge of the cliff. But instead of kicking Isaiah's hand away, he reached down and pulled him up to safety. Lucas grabbed for Isaiah's arm and pulled his friend the rest of the way away from the ledge. Then Biddle-Bratt turned to Slappy and began to march toward him.

"What are you doing?" Slappy asked.

Biddle-Bratt glared at the dummy. "I didn't hurt my parents," he screamed in rage. "You did!" Then he grabbed Slappy and threw him off the edge of the cliff. Suddenly, a loud moan came from somewhere deep within Nathan's body. He opened his mouth, and in a rush, the ghostly vapor of Harold's burned body came spilling out.

Nathan finally had his body back. "It's real," the English teacher said, patting himself to make sure. "I'm real."

Everyone turned and saw Harold's ghostly figure standing in the snow. A moment later, the ghostly figures of his parents appeared behind him. Harold turned, stepping toward them. Just as the three Biddles embraced in a hug, the trio suddenly disappeared. It was finally time for them to move on, together.

"It's over," Nora said. "It's finally over."

CHAPTER FORTY-FIVE

Before he'd inherited the old hunting lodge in Port Lawrence, things had not been going well for Nathan Bratt. He had lost his teaching job, he didn't have enough money to make rent, he had been trying to write a book (which was not going well), and even worse, his beloved dog, Fifi, had been hit by a car and died. Sweet Fifi, a kind and loving white poodle, had been Nathan's best friend. Without her, he had nothing and no one. Life just couldn't get any worse.

And then, one day, things began to look up.

Someone had knocked at his apartment door, and when Nathan answered, he'd found a lawyer on the other side. "Are you Nathan Bratt?"

"Unfortunately," Nathan answered. He was pretty sure the lawyer was there to kick him out, since he'd avoided sending in his rent payment for one too many weeks.

"Can I come in?" Nathan widened the door, reluctantly letting the lawyer enter. "My firm has represented the interests of the Ephraim Bratt estate for many decades. It took significant effort to determine the line of succession and locate you."

"Ephraim Bratt . . ." Nathan said. "Wait, you're not here to evict me?"

"You have inherited your great-grandfather's property. It's a substantial estate."

"Are you serious?" Nathan asked.

"Yes, Mr. Bratt. It's your lucky day."

It turned out, Nathan's good luck didn't end up being that lucky, after all. There was the whole ghost-possessing-his-body thing, the evil dummy, and then the haunted scrapbook. The inherited house wasn't lucky—it was a curse.

Classic Nathan.

But now, finally, Nathan's bad luck was over. He was back in his body, the ghost and dummy were gone, and the scrapbook had been destroyed. Nathan staggered into his house after returning from the mountain snowstorm adventure. He collapsed to his knees in the middle of the old Biddle living room and released a deep, heavy sigh. Then he began to laugh. Nathan realized, gratefully, that he finally had the perfect story to tell.

"This," he said aloud, his voice echoing through the living room, "will make a great book."

Four weeks later, Nathan had written most of a draft detailing a fictionalized version of the adventures he'd had since arriving in Port Lawrence. All that was left to write was the ending. "For the teens of Port Seymore," Nathan read aloud as he typed the beginning of his epilogue, "the haunted clouds hanging over them had finally parted."

If Nathan considered things more carefully, however, he would realize that—with *his* luck—the haunted clouds would surely be back. But still, he wrote on until he reached the ending he so desperately *wanted* to see:

The teens and their parents had defeated the evil that was the wooden dummy, Snappy. And they all knew none of it would have been possible without their intrepid leader, Nicholas Back.

Nathan grinned as he wrote himself into the hero line of the story.

Now all Back wanted was to see the town flourish under the sun of a new day. A new beginning for all of Port Seymore.

He leaned back in his seat, deeply satisfied. Then he composed an email to Scholarly Press, attached the draft of his manuscript, and hit SEND. A new beginning, indeed.

A few days later, Nathan was chatting with Ben while his new pal mounted the taxidermic body of Nathan's dead poodle, Fifi, on the wall of the living room alongside all the other taxidermy creatures. "A little to the left," Nathan said, gesturing to the spot he meant. "I want Fifi level with all the other heads."

As Ben secured the poodle into place on the wall, Nathan told him, "Fifi was my grandmother's poodle. On her deathbed, I promised I would care for Fifi as if she was my own. And I did. And Fifi repaid me in spades. She saw me through a lot of hard times. Really, really hard times." He glanced up at Ben, suddenly brightening. "It took being possessed by a kid that you and your friends killed to finally change my luck for the better!"

"Look"—Ben sighed—"you keep bringing up everything that happened."

"I'm just trying to piece it all together," Nathan explained.

"And we're just trying to put it all behind us," Ben reminded him.

"You're right, you're right." Nathan nodded. "All I'm trying to say is that I have a house. I have friends like you! And now, I finished my book!"

"Book?"

"It might sound familiar," Nathan said with a smile. "It's a tale of intrigue and murder in a small town. Like Stephen King's *Carrie* meets Stephen King's *The Shining* . . . with a touch of levity."

"Wait . . ." Ben said, alarmed. Nathan was writing a *book* about all that had happened?

"It's fine," Nathan said to reassure him. "It's *fiction*." Then he paused. "Hey, can I pay you for this project next month? I'm a little light in the bank account right now. Teacher's salary."

Ben shook his head. "Don't worry about it."

CHAPTER FORTY-SIX

Ever since their adventures with Slappy out on the mountain, things had slowly returned to a new normal in Port Lawrence. Isaiah's arm was healing faster than anyone had expected it to. James and Sam were back on again . . . and so were Margot and Lucas, whose budding new relationship was off to a strong start. Though they were an unlikely couple, it seemed to be working out surprisingly well. Isabella was still pining after Isaiah . . . who was totally oblivious to her attention, since he was still frustrated Lucas had gotten to Margot before he had a chance to tell his old friend how he really felt. And things were becoming even more complicated now that Margot's mom was going back to Seattle, and she wanted her daughter to join her there. For good. The twisted love square was about to get even more knotted.

Margot still hadn't made up her mind about whether she wanted to move or not, and she knew she had to scope out the city. So she convinced her friends to come hang out with her in Seattle for the weekend, to check it out.

The friends were gearing up for a big road trip and a fun weekend away. But Lucas wasn't totally sold on the idea. It wasn't just that he didn't *want* Margot to move; he was also reluctant to leave his mom after everything that had happened.

"Hey," Nora said, knocking on his door. "Your friends are all downstairs waiting on you. What's up?"

"Maybe I should stay," he said, glancing up at his mom. "What if you need me? What if something happens?"

Nora sat on the bed next to her son. "Lucas, it's okay. I'm okay. Things are okay now. Even . . . good." She paused, sensing his nerves. "I know this has been scary. And I bet it still feels so close. But as someone who has lived in fear for so long, I am telling you it's safe for you to go and have fun and live your life."

"It's hard to shake off everything we went through," he told her quietly.

"I know," Nora nodded. "I'm not saying it's easy. And I'm sorry that everything you're feeling is my fault." She nudged him. "But please, go have fun with your friends."

As the group piled into James's Jeep outside the Harbor Stop, Nathan walked past them to grab a coffee. "Hey, where are you guys headed?" he called out.

"Weekend in Seattle," Isabella yelled back.

"Seattle!" Nathan said, grinning. "I know it well. Land of the ten-dollar coffees." Just as he was about to step inside the shop, his phone rang. Nathan glanced down and muttered to himself, "A New York number . . . it's a call from New York!" He clicked ACCEPT, then said, "Hello, Nathan Bratt speaking."

"Mr. Bratt!" chirped a voice on the other end. "It's Ann Macy at Scholarly Press. We've received your manuscript, and I was wondering if you had a second to chat?"

"Of course!"

"First of all," the editor began, "we love the direction you've taken with this. New horror, so now. So cutting edge. My boss is very interested in this book. There's just one . . . tiny thing."

Nathan froze, waiting to hear what the one *tiny* thing could be.

"It needs a new ending," the editor finished.

"You want me to write a whole new ending?"

"Not new," Ann said. "More. This book wants a satisfying finale that's unexpected but also digs deeper into explaining Snappy's backstory. We need the *why*, the *how*, and the *who*. You understand? Honestly, Mr. Bratt, I am so excited about this project. It's just one of those once-in-a-lifetime manuscripts to me. If we can get this right, this is so clearly a book series."

Nathan hung up. He couldn't believe it. If he could write a new ending, he had a possible book *series* deal? *Yes!* A book series screamed money.

How hard could it be to come up with a new ending?

Later that night, Nathan sat at his desk with his laptop open in front of him. "Okay, Fifi," he said, looking up for inspiration at the stuffed dog now hanging on the wall above him. "Here we go. Let's find that new ending. The perfect twist." He shook his hands, ready to release the words that were surely ready to spill out. But nothing spilled. "Come on, man," he growled to himself. "You've got this. So close. Fire up the old imagination. No pressure." He glanced at the stack of bills and late notices on the edge of his desk. He really needed the money from a book sale. Like, bad. "Okay, a little bit of pressure."

He began to type. Suddenly, he had an idea. "I got it! I got it!" The words spilled out like water, flowing from him as if he were possessed with the ghost of Shakespeare or something. "Oh, that's great," he mused.

Just as Nathan was about to finish, his phone rang.

"Hey," Ann the editor chirped out from the other end. "Just checking in. Have you had a blast of inspiration yet?"

"Yes, actually," Nathan said proudly. "Yes. Okay, new ending—"

"Just as long as we don't find out they're all ghosts in the end," Ann said with a laugh. "That's, like, been done, okay?"

Nathan's mouth snapped closed. "Uh . . . totally," he said. He slammed his finger down on the delete key and erased everything he'd written that night. Pages and pages of new ending that now needed to be rewritten. "You know what? I'll just let you read it."

"Great!" Ann said happily. "Nathan, I really think you could be the next Stephen King. But you need to get this ending to me as soon as humanly possible. Or else my boss is going to have to move on."

Nathan paled. "You think he'd move on?"

Ann barked out a laugh. "I *know* he'll move on. So get that ending over to me right away."

Nathan was stuck. Blocked. Ending-less. He climbed into his car and drove around aimlessly, listening to his favorite writing podcast.

"On today's episode of *Let the Write One In*, we're discussing endings," the podcast host said soothingly. Nathan reached into his bag of fries and grabbed a mouthful, ready to gobble up whatever the podcast host was throwing down. "Ideas are often depicted as a light bulb coming on. Why? Because true creation comes from darkness. You cannot create unless you allow yourself to sit in that darkness, the blackness, the nothingness we have before the big idea." Nathan nodded eagerly. "The perfect twist! This darkness is where imagination is born. So, you out there listening . . . what are you willing to do?"

Nathan looked up the road and suddenly spotted a sign that read: MOUNT SEYMORE—20 MILES.

He considered this. Maybe there was a reason he was driving in the direction he was. Suddenly, he had an idea. Should he revisit the mountains where they'd dumped Slappy? He smiled at himself in the rearview mirror and then pressed his foot down on the gas pedal. "That would be a twist."

CHAPTER FORTY-SEVEN

Almost as soon as they got to Seattle, Lucas was acting off. He was fidgety, quiet, and he didn't seem remotely happy to be there. "Are you okay?" Margot asked while they waited in a long line of people who were all queued up to buy the latest fad pastry.

"This line is crazy," Lucas grumbled. He was worried sick about his mom, and he couldn't believe that instead of being there for her, he was waiting in an endless line for overpriced baked goods. Didn't people have better things to do with their time? "How good could a doughnut actually be?" He rolled his eyes and looked right at Margot. "Don't you find Seattle kind of depressing?"

"No," Margot said with a shrug, annoyed that he was trying to ruin this whole experience for everyone. "It's just cloudy."

"All I know is that when I run the Harbor Stop, I'm going to have totally okay doughnuts that you can get without waiting in line for two hours."

Margot stared back at him. She snorted. "You want to run the Harbor Stop?"

"Yeah, of course." Lucas shrugged. Margot laughed but

stopped when she realized Lucas was being serious and she sounded overly judgmental about Lucas's life dream. But Lucas had already caught her drift; he could see Margot didn't think very highly of his dream *or* his mom's business. He scoffed, "Well, if you move here, you can eat fancy doughnuts all the time."

After Margot and Lucas got their doughnuts, the whole group headed out to a party Margot's cousin had told her about. "First big city party," James whooped as they made their way inside. The place was pretty dead, just a bunch of college kids hanging out chatting. "Why did I think there would be dance music?"

It wasn't exactly what any of them had been expecting, but it did seem pretty chill. Maybe this was how parties looked in big cities? James grinned. "We can do this," he told the others. "We've been haunted by cameras and masks and actual ghosts. We've explored crumbling alternate realities."

"Somehow," Isabella mused quietly, "those things were all less intimidating."

"Way less," Isaiah agreed.

"Do we want to do this?" Lucas said, feeling *very* unsure. This whole Seattle vibe was one hundred percent *not* his thing. If this was what Margot wanted, they were obviously much more different than he had realized. Maybe he should just step back and let her go for it. Who was he to crush someone else's dream? Especially someone as special as Margot.

But Margot was clearly on a different page altogether. She was trying to solve every awkward situation by jumping into the experience with two feet. "I should go look for my cousin," she said, and then she plunged into the terrifying party.

Isaiah and Isabella stood together at the edge of the room. Things had been weird between them. For a while, after all the Harold scrapbook stuff happened, they'd kinda been vibing. But lately, not so much. Isabella felt like she was turning invisible again, slowly but surely.

Isaiah finally leaned into Isabella and asked, "So, you don't hate me?"

"Why would I hate you?"

"I know I wasn't really texting you back for a bit there," Isaiah said, flashing an apologetic smile. "I just—I guess—I didn't know what to say."

"You didn't know how to reply to 'Want to hang out?'" Isabella said skeptically.

"I've been trying to figure out how to tell my dad I might not want to play football anymore, and school has been—"

"It's fine," Isabella assured him, and she meant it. She wasn't going to force him into something. When he figured out she was worth it, he'd see her again. "We're fine."

"I think you're really cool," Isaiah said with a grin.

"I am," she said softly.

Across the room, Lucas was miserable. "Hey, I was looking for you," Margot said, sidling up beside him.

"I think I'm gonna go," Lucas said with a deep sigh. "I just really don't want to be here."

"You're not even trying," Margot said.

"All I've been doing is trying," Lucas snapped back. "I don't know why everyone acts like 'moving on' is so easy."

"Not easy doesn't mean not worth it," Margot pointed out.

"I'm just not where you're at, okay?" Lucas spat at her. His mom had almost died, and she was all he had left. How could Margot not understand that he was worried about his mom? "This trip was for you."

"This trip was for *us*," Margot argued. "To help me figure out if I should move here."

"I know you're gonna leave," Lucas said. Everyone left. Everyone he'd ever loved had left him—except his mom. And now he'd abandoned her to come to this stupid Seattle party? No. So not worth it. Margot was going to abandon him, too, so he might as well cut ties before he got hurt even worse.

"So that means you're just out?" Margot snapped.

"You're the one leaving." He shrugged. "I like Port Lawrence, okay? I know that. I like my life there, and the people there, and that's where I should be. That's what I care about right now. I shouldn't have come."

"Maybe not," Margot said. "And maybe we're not meant to be together."

"Okay," Lucas said, then he spun around and walked out of the party, leaving Margot staring after him. He'd made his decision. He was going home. Right now. He had finally realized that he and Margot would never be on the same page. So it was time to close the book.

CHAPTER FORTY-EIGHT

Back in Port Lawrence, Nathan dumped Slappy's pieces out onto the floor in front of his fireplace. He took a deep breath. *Was this the right choice?* Well, it was too late to change his mind now, so he might as well make the most of his decision.

He reached into Slappy's jacket pocket and found the card that had the spell written on it. Holding it gingerly in his hand, Nathan paced back and forth across the living room. He wanted his ending, his book deal, his dream, but he knew there was no going back if he did what he was pretty sure he *needed* to do to make all his dreams come true. Finally, he came to a decision. "This is the only way."

He held up the card and read aloud: *"Karru Marri Odonna Loma Molonu Karrano."* He took a step back, waiting for the magic to happen. But nothing.

Then, suddenly, Slappy's pieces began to move. Slowly, they slid into place and Slappy fused back to wholeness. While Nathan watched, mesmerized, Slappy turned his head and looked right at him. "What took you so long?"

"I," Nathan began. "I need—"

"You need an ending," Slappy said simply. "And I'm going to give you the greatest ending of all time."

Just then, Nathan heard a familiar sound. He looked up just in time to see Fifi's tail wag. "Fifi?" Nathan gasped. His dog was alive! "It's a miracle!" Slappy had already made him *very* happy indeed.

Late that night, Nathan marched across the old Biddle property. He was following Fifi, who was leading him *somewhere*. Fifi suddenly stopped and began to dig. "We're going to dig?" he asked the dog, feeling a tad uncertain. This seemed like a terrible idea.

But suddenly, Fifi's eyes began to glow red and she opened her mouth to reveal her teeth, which had become sharp fangs.

"Oh my god," Nathan said, stumbling backward. What had happened to his sweet Fifi? She growled at him, until Nathan stepped forward to help her dig. "Okay, okay," he said, pushing his shovel into the dirt.

He and Fifi dug until they hit something solid. It was a large, rectangular box. Nathan dragged it out of the hole and pulled it across the property and into the living room of his house. Once inside, he could see the inscription on the side of the box: KANDUU.

Slappy, propped up in a chair, watched as Nathan studied the box. It was now very clear that this *box* was actually a *coffin*.

"I don't know about this," Nathan said, partly to himself and partly to Slappy.

"Nothing to know," Slappy told him. "You need this."

Fifi bared her teeth at Nathan, snarling. As her eyes began to glow red again, Nathan dropped down to his knees. He flipped open the coffin lid, his eyes squeezed tightly shut. Following orders from Slappy, Nathan reached into the coffin and felt around for what he was searching for. His hand emerged a moment later with a small white card clutched between his fingers. As he began to read the incantation on the card, Nathan suddenly got a horrifying vision: people running and screaming, all with dummy faces, as if everyone in the world had been turned into Slappy. He dropped the card in shock.

"What are you doing?" Slappy demanded.

"I just saw—I just saw—is that the ending?" Nathan asked, shocked. "Is that . . . real?"

"Read," Slappy ordered.

"Because that, like, doesn't seem good," Nathan said. What he'd seen was terrifying. That ending was too horrifying to consider. "Maybe we could tone it down just a bit—"

"Read!"

Nathan's eyes snapped back to the card, and he began to read aloud, *"Aldu Meindu Haldoom Zandratz."* He recited the last word, then glanced up at Slappy just in time to see the doll wilt and collapse into a heap. As Nathan inspected the lifeless puppet, he suddenly heard a noise behind him. He spun around, realizing the noise was coming from *inside* the coffin.

His eyes went wide with terror as a dusty, horrifying skeleton emerged from the wooden box. As Nathan watched, unable to look away, the skeleton began to transform into the reborn body of the magician Kanduu. As Nathan had read the incantation, his soul had finally been released from Slappy's long-possessed form, and had now, finally, been returned to its rightful body.

Nathan stared in disbelief. The dead body in the coffin . . . had come back to life?

Suddenly, there was a knock at the door. Ben strolled inside and called out, "Hey, Nathan, I know it's late. But I've gotta talk to you about this book you've been writing." He stepped into the living room and spotted Kanduu. "Who are you?" he asked.

In response, Kanduu reached into his pocket and pulled out an old military field guide. He began to read from it, *"Adanna Meenu Sanara Kudarash."*

As soon as Kanduu had finished saying the magic words, Ben began to freeze up. In less than five seconds, the transformation was complete. Ben had been turned into a dummy.

KANDUU

CHAPTER FORTY-NINE

*O*n a battlefield in the middle of the countryside, a man named Rupert Campbell was about to die. He'd been shot in the stomach, and blood was pouring out of him. But just as he was about to close his eyes for the last time, a bomb exploded on the ground in front of him, knocking open the wall of the trench, and revealing the secret opening to a hidden cave.

Rupert fell into the cave, moaning as he rolled to a stop in the quiet blackness. Feeling around in the dark, the soldier searched for a miracle. He had mere minutes left, and he didn't want to die alone in the dark. Rupert suddenly noticed that the trail of blood spilling out of him was trickling into some kind of carving on the floor, filled with oil. Using his lighter, Rupert pressed a flame to the liquid. As it caught, the fire spread through the trench. He watched, mystified, as a wall covered in carvings was illuminated before him in the light from the flames.

Studying the carvings, Rupert began to read aloud: "Moori Azana Kanduu."

All of a sudden, the blood that had spilled from his body onto the floor of the cave began to pool together, reversing back up and into his open wound. As Rupert scrabbled to pull aside his shirt, he watched the wound close up completely. He'd been healed.

Confused, Rupert stepped toward the wall. What was this magic he'd found? He carefully wrote everything into his field journal, not wanting to leave any of the magic behind. Just as he scribbled down the last bits, Rupert took in the drawing at the center of the wall. It was a large spire, built out of layers and layers of human bodies.

A few years later, the man once known as Rupert made his way across a field in a small North American town. He was heading toward a very specific traveling carnival. Stepping inside a tent at the edge of the grounds, the former soldier spotted a wooden puppet.

"Wood from coffins adds to their aura," said a voice behind him. "Do you like my work?" The man stepped forward and introduced himself. "I'm Franz Mahar."

"Kanduu," the former soldier said. He'd changed his name in honor of the incantation that had healed him and saved his life on the battlefield that day.

"Oh, the magician," Mahar said with a slight bow. "I've heard of you."

"I'm not a magician," Kanduu said quickly.

"No?" Mahar said, curious. "Then what are you?"

Kanduu turned to one of the featureless wooden puppets inside the tent and began to speak. "Alem Nadri Meena Nari!"

The puppet suddenly came to life, pulling itself upright as it turned its head to Mahar. "Hello, Papa," said the puppet.

"A magician is someone who stands on a corner and tricks people for money," Kanduu explained. "My magic is real."

Mahar nodded slowly. "I see that."

"This carnival is a failure," Kanduu said simply. "But I can help you change that."

Mahar considered this. "They would flock from all around to see you," he said, realizing what Kanduu was offering. Fame, glory, riches, crowds.

"In exchange," Kanduu told the puppet-maker, "I need you to build something for me."

"Anything," promised Mahar, not realizing that he'd just made a deal with the devil.

A year later, Mahar's long dream of success had come true. But at what price? He glanced across the field just outside his carnival's grounds, taking in the large wooden spire he'd been building out of wood for Kanduu. He still wasn't sure what the spire would be used for, but it was Kanduu's one wish.

With a deep breath, Mahar walked toward the area where Kanduu was performing his evening show. Mahar watched from the darkened edge of the stage as the magician performed his incantations, aided by a volunteer from the audience. When the person onstage with Kanduu turned, Mahar gasped in terror. The person standing beside him had been turned into a dummy.

Mahar looked out at the crowd. To his horror, every single person in the audience had succumbed to the same fate. "You've turned them all into puppets?" Mahar hissed at Kanduu.

"For the ritual," Kanduu explained. "There's a reason I chose your carnival, Mahar. You're a maker of puppets. Now you can become a puppet master."

Kanduu spun and walked off the stage, leaving Mahar to wonder aloud, "What have I done?"

Several nights later, Kanduu sat inside the tent within the carnival grounds that served as his study. He was staring at a miniature model of the spire sitting on the tabletop, dreaming of the future it promised him. Mahar entered the study, holding a case in his hands. He'd brought Kanduu a gift, something he'd been working on especially for the magician.

"Hello, old friend," Kanduu said, sounding excited. "Tonight is the night. Are you ready?"

"Yes, yes," Mahar answered. "I am. I've put a lot of thought into it, actually." He placed the case on the table, then clicked it open. When he lifted the lid off the case, it revealed what was inside: a perfect, intricate ventriloquist dummy. "A small gift, to mark this special occasion."

Kanduu studied the puppet in the case, amused. "This is the doll I brought to life the day we met." He could tell his friend had put much time and care into perfecting the doll, adding details until it was almost lifelike in its design. "It's perfect."

"I'm glad you like him," Mahar said, reaching into his pocket to pull out a small card. "Because it's your turn to be the puppet."

Kanduu stared at his friend, confused. Mahar was holding Kanduu's own incantation card. He had stolen it from him!

Just as Mahar said, "Loma," Kanduu reached for a knife and plunged it into the puppet-maker. Mahar continued to talk through the pain. "Molonu . . ."

"Stop!" Kanduu begged. "Please!"

With one more gasp, Mahar finished the spell. "Karrano."

Suddenly, Kanduu's soul was transferred from his human body into the wooden puppet sitting within the case. The dummy's eyes opened as Kanduu's body fell to the ground, lifeless. With his dying breath, Mahar closed the case as the incantation card he'd been reading from fell inside and was sealed away, alongside the magician's soul.

PART SEVEN

— *The Spire* —

WELCOME TO HORRORLAND

CHAPTER FIFTY

"Should we brunch?" James asked, yawning when he woke up at Sarah's apartment the next morning. Unlike Lucas, he'd had a blast during their weekend in Seattle and was in no hurry to get back to the middle of nowhere when he could be in a thriving city. "There's nowhere in Port Lawrence to brunch, and in Seattle it seems like there's *only* brunch."

"My mom's out getting bagels," Margot said, glancing up from her phone. She'd been staring at her screen all morning, waiting for Lucas to reach out. He'd left a note the night before, telling her that he was taking a bus home. He hadn't texted since he'd ditched her at the party, and she couldn't believe he'd just *leave* like that—just like her mom had. He had to know that would kill her.

James sighed. "Or . . . we could have bagels."

Isaiah glanced at Margot, noticing that she was hurriedly stuffing her things into her bag. "Maybe we should head home," he suggested. Even if this was just about Lucas, he hated seeing Margot this upset. He'd suck it up and do what he needed to do if it meant she could be happy again. "After bagels."

Margot glanced at him gratefully. Isaiah had always been good at interpreting her emotions. And he clearly knew that what she needed right now was to get home. "Has anyone heard from Lucas since last night?" she asked the others.

"Yeah, after you fell asleep," Isabella said. "He's fine."

"So he texted you guys back," Margot noted.

Isaiah draped an arm around her shoulders. "I'm sorry," he whispered.

Margot pulled away from him and began storming angrily around the room. "He just left me. *Left* me! Just 'Good-bye, I'm going home.' No 'Sorry we had a fight' or anything? Just 'Good-bye, I guess it's over.' I mean, who does that?"

No one knew what to say. Finally, James said, "Apparently . . . Lucas?" The others gave him a look, and James shrugged. "She asked!"

"It's fine," Margot snapped. She wasn't actually looking for answers. And it was clear nothing was going to make her feel better about this. "We're too different. Right? Lucas and I are just really different people. Maybe I should just stay in Seattle and never go back."

Miles away in Port Lawrence, Lucas wandered home toward the Harbor Stop. Along the way, he silenced another call from Margot, not wanting to talk to her just yet. He didn't know what to say. He just needed some space and time to think. Pressing into the café, Lucas noticed it was much quieter than usual for midday. "Mom?" he called out.

But there was no response. He ran upstairs, pushing open the door to their apartment. "Mom? Where is everyone?"

"Hey, kid," a voice behind him said. Lucas turned and found his dad, Dennis, standing there.

"Dad?" Lucas said. "How—"

"How is this possible?" Dennis asked with a small smile. "It's a long story, but you know the Witness Protection Program? Well, I was in it. I know how crazy that sounds. But it's true; I was a government witness. Even your mom didn't know. I couldn't tell her."

Lucas shook his head, not able to believe it. But this was his dad, all right, standing just feet in front of him. "We had a funeral," he said, choking back the tears that wanted to fall. "I finally let you go . . ."

"Don't be mad at him," Lucas's mom said, stepping up behind his dad. "He didn't have a choice."

"It was that or go to prison," Dennis said with a shrug. "Look, the trial is over. I'm back. And I'm never leaving again." He reached out his hand to Lucas, eager to pull him in for a hug. "Come on, son. Let's make up for lost time. What do you say you and I go for a ride? Put everything behind us."

Lucas reached out and took his dad's hand. But as soon as he grasped it in his own, Dennis melted away, leaving Kanduu standing in the spot where his father had been moments before. Nothing that had just happened was real. It was all part of Kanduu's spell.

Before Kanduu turned to walk away, he glanced one last time at Lucas and Nora, both of whom had been turned into dummies.

Kanduu exited the café and walked toward town. He had more work to do.

CHAPTER FIFTY-ONE

James pulled his Jeep in front of Margot's and Isaiah's houses. He'd already dropped off Isabella, and as soon as Margot was out of the car, James held his best friend back for a second.

"You just have to do it, Isaiah," James told him.

"Do what?"

"Talk to Margot," James said. He'd watched his friend staring at Margot like a lovesick puppy all weekend. Now that he'd finally broken up with Allison, he could finally try to make something happen with Margot. Only trouble was, Lucas had gotten to her first. But now that there was trouble brewing between them, this could be Isaiah's chance to finally clear the air.

"Lucas's seat in the car isn't even cold yet," Isaiah grumbled.

"Dude," James groaned. "Life is about taking risks. Point is, the seat's empty. Now go take a risk for once in your life. Don't play it safe."

Isaiah hopped out of the car and waved after him as James drove away. James was probably right. He had to say something, and if she wasn't interested, well, then at least he'd know he didn't have a shot. He called out, "Margot, wait."

"What?" Margot said, spinning around. "What is it?"

He took her hand in his and she looked down at their linked hands, confused. "Um . . . what are you doing?" She pulled away.

"James," Isaiah said, raking his hand through his hair. "Freaking James. I'm sorry." He turned to walk away.

"Do you want to talk to me about whatever just happened there?" Margot asked gently.

He turned back and looked at her. She was right. She deserved to hear his truth. "Here's the thing," he began. "I know you're not with Lucas right now. And before you make any decisions about what comes next, I want to tell you the truth. I have feelings for you." He exhaled loudly. "And it's so hard to say because I've known you forever. We grew up together, and I know everything about you. I know that right after we talk, you're going to write about this in your journal and use at least three words that are unnecessary but describe this moment better than I ever could—"

"Unexpected, overwhelming, intense," she cut in.

"See?" he said, grinning. "And I just want to give this a shot— give *us* a shot. Before we lose our chance."

Margot was stunned. This was what she'd been waiting for, for so long. She'd wanted to hear Isaiah say something exactly like this for over ten years. But now was not *when* she wanted to hear it. The past twenty-four hours had been too much, and she couldn't process yet another change. "I don't know what to say . . ."

"Don't worry," Isaiah said with a shrug. An I-don't-know was a whole lot better than a no. "You don't have to say anything now. Just think about it."

Kanduu was waiting, ready to greet each of the teens when they returned from Seattle. He'd nearly reached his goal, and now he just needed a few more people for his ritual. He was ready to offer each of them their greatest desire. And when they accepted, he'd take his payment in the form of their soul, turning them into dummies in the process.

Kanduu lured Isaiah with the full-ride football scholarship he'd always wished for.

Then he posed as Sam and offered James a perfect, Insta-worthy promposal.

He set up Isabella so her mom was waiting to greet her with a big, happy, proud smile on her face when her daughter got home.

And Margot arrived home to find that her parents were back together, trying to make their marriage work again.

Now he just had to see if they would fall for his traps . . .

Isaiah was conflicted about how things had gone with Margot when he told her he had feelings for her. But when he entered his house to find a college scout standing there with a scholarship offer, he thought maybe his day was turning around. Isaiah smiled and reached for the pen to sign the contract, but it was then that he noticed the cast had disappeared from his arm. That could only mean one thing: None of this was real. It was all a fantasy.

Isaiah fled to Margot's house. He burst into the room as she was about to walk into her parents' embrace. "It's not real!" he screamed. Margot's confused expression transformed into terror when she turned to see Kanduu and her Slappified dad where her happy parents had been standing.

Margot and Isaiah raced out of the house just as James's Jeep pulled up outside. "Get in!" James cried, screeching to a stop.

The friends hopped in the backseat, relieved to discover that James and Isabella had also figured out Kanduu's traps before it was too late.

Once they had left Margot's and Isaiah's houses in the distance, Margot looked out of the car's rear window and saw Slappified versions of all of their parents standing with Kanduu in the middle of the street. "Who is that guy?" she asked the others.

"What did he do to our parents?" Isaiah asked.

"And how do we undo it?" James said.

"Lucas was right. He knew it wasn't over. That's why he was so upset on the trip," Margot said. "We have to find him before the same thing happens to him."

They sped to the Harbor Stop, running inside to try to find Lucas. But the place was completely empty—not a soul was inside. But there were signs that people had been there recently: a half-eaten sandwich on a table, a purse, someone's cell phone.

"Not that it wasn't already creepy," Isabella said softly. "Now it's getting creepier."

Just then, they heard the sound of Lucas's motorbike. They all ran outside, eager to get to him before Kanduu could. But Lucas had already zipped off, heading across town, so the four of them piled into the Jeep and raced after him.

It quickly became clear that Lucas was heading for the high school. "Why's he here on a Sunday?" James asked. "I didn't miss the SAT again, did I?"

Just as Lucas was about to pull into the parking lot, the Jeep finally caught up to him. Margot rolled down her window and called, "Lucas! Wait!"

Lucas stopped the engine and climbed off his bike. Slowly, he removed his helmet and turned . . . but the others could immediately see that Kanduu had gotten to their friend first. Lucas's jaw unhinged, then he opened his mouth in a silent scream. Moments later, the Slappified versions of all their parents appeared out of nowhere, descending on the car like a pack of zombies. They opened the car doors and dragged their kids out screaming.

They tried to resist, but the dummy versions of their parents had some kind of superhuman strength. While the four friends tried to fight back, their parents dragged them toward the football field. And that's when they got their first look at the huge wooden spire that had been built right in the center. Townspeople, all of them in dummy form, climbed the ramps surrounding the tower, taking their places around the wooden structure.

"What the hell is that?" Isaiah screamed as they were shoved into a tent at the edge of the field. "Dad!" he shouted, trying to get through to his dad. Ben seemed to be in some sort of trance. "Please, what are you doing? Wake up!"

"He can't hear you," said a voice from the back of the tent.

The four of them peered into the darkness and saw Nathan step out of the shadows. "They're all under a spell," he said with an apologetic smile. "If you fall for the fantasy, he turns you into a living dummy he can control."

Margot gaped at him. "So you're saying everyone in town has been turned into a 'living dummy,' except for you?"

James gave him a look. "Yeah . . . that's not suspicious at all."

"I made a deal," Nathan said with a shrug. "It's a complicated story."

Isabella couldn't believe this. "You brought Slappy back, didn't you?"

Before Nathan could answer, Kanduu entered the tent with Fifi by his side. The poodle's eyes glowed red, and she flashed her razor-sharp fangs at them. "He did a lot more than that," Kanduu said softly. "He freed me. It's good to see you all again."

"That voice," Isaiah said, recognizing it immediately.

"It's Slappy," James said.

"Yes," Kanduu purred. "I was trapped in the body of that undignified doll for more years than I care to count."

"You were behind all of this," Margot said. "Everything that has happened to us. We thought it was Harold. We thought it was Slappy. But it was you all along."

Kanduu nodded. "It was me all along." He began to recite an incantation. *"Neni Omina Zargat."* In the next instant, the tent melted away and the group was suddenly standing with Kanduu in the trench, in the moments just before he—Rupert—was shot by enemy warfare.

"It's like the visions in the scrapbook," Isabella noted, realizing that Kanduu had the ability to transport them anywhere, to see anything. He had indescribable power.

Kanduu explained, "We were in a country we didn't belong in, for something that wasn't ours to begin with. I had seen too many lives lost. And I was done fighting." He changed the scene, and suddenly they were standing in the temple with him, just after he'd been shot. Kanduu went on, "They had taught us the local languages before the war, and I was able to sound out the inscriptions on the wall. I almost died in this temple, but I was reborn instead. The word that healed me became my name and my purpose."

The magician stepped forward, running his hand across the image of the spire on the wall of the cave within the vision. "What is written on these walls will save us all. These are the magical spells that bring back monsters, ghosts, demons, curses—every type of horror known to man."

"And that's a *good* thing?" Isaiah asked.

"Don't you see?" Kanduu said, spinning around. "War. The way humans treat each other. In the absence of true horrors, humans created their own. And they were far worse. People need monsters, or they *become* monsters." He took a deep breath, then smiled. "That's why I'm going to release all of these horrors at once. By performing the Ritual of the Spire." He pointed to the scene carved into the wall.

James leaned in for a closer look. "There are bodies on that spire thingy!"

Suddenly, the scene dissolved again and they were back in Kanduu's tent on the football field. Now the magician was standing beside the small model of the spire, alongside Nathan. "One thousand souls need to be sacrificed for the greater good," Kanduu said.

Nathan's head snapped up at this. "Wait, what?"

"There won't ever be wars again when I give people something to really be scared of," Kanduu explained.

Margot shook her head. "You're just trying to justify inflicting the horror you went through on everyone else."

"To save the world!" Kanduu exclaimed.

"No, to *punish* the world for what you went through," Margot argued.

Kanduu grew angry and blurted, "I thought you would understand why I was doing this, after all you've been through."

"We understand what you're doing is *wrong* because of what we've been through," Isaiah said.

"Then you understand nothing," Kanduu spat. "Now your death won't be a sacrifice. Just a death." He strolled to the door of the tent, calling out as he walked outside, "Kill them."

"Kill them?" Nathan asked in disbelief.

Kanduu gestured to the dog standing just outside the tent. "I was talking to the dog."

Fifi entered the tent, her red eyes flashing. Her vampire fangs were dripping with saliva as she began to snarl and move toward the group. Suddenly, Nathan jumped out of the shadows and stabbed

Fifi through the heart with a wooden stake. "I'm so sorry, Fifi," he wailed. "I'm so sorry, but it's not really you! I can't let you kill them!"

Nathan swept the poodle up into his arms as she expired, *again*. But this time, she turned into a poof of dust. "I did *not* realize he was going to sacrifice the whole town," Nathan said, turning to face the others.

"What did you think all those people, our families, were doing up on that spire?" Isabella yelled back.

"I don't know!" Nathan shrugged. "A ritual can mean a lot of different things."

"He's going to kill our parents," Margot said. "And Lucas."

"And everyone we know," James added.

"Oh my god," Nathan wailed. "If I knew this was going to happen, I never would have done it."

"Why *did* you do it?" Isaiah asked.

"I needed an ending to my book," Nathan explained. He hung his head. "That sounds even more pathetic and self-serving when I say it out loud."

"I can't believe you did this," Isabella snapped.

"I *can* believe it," James cut in.

"I can, too," Nathan said sadly. "I'm a good enough writer to know I'm *not* a good enough writer. So I cheated. You ever do something so dumb, but don't realize how dumb in the moment because you're blinded by your own desire? Apparently, it runs in the family. All the way back to my great-great-grandfather, Franz Mahar. He was the first one to make a deal with Kanduu." Nathan shook his head. "Ironically, he's also the one who figured out how to stop him."

"Stop him?" Isaiah asked suddenly. "Wait, how did Mahar stop Kanduu?"

Nathan walked over to Kanduu's desk and picked up the magician's journal. He began flipping through the pages, flashing the incantations at the others. "According to Mahar's manuscripts, he used his magic against him. He was his partner for many years. He learned all of Kanduu's secrets."

"But how, exactly?" Isabella asked.

"I don't know," Nathan said. "You would have to ask him."

"Great advice," James muttered. "We'll just bring back the dead guy. Good thing you're so good at bringing people back from the grave."

Margot and Isaiah exchanged a look, and it was clear to both of them that they had the same idea. It might not work, but at least they had a plan to *try*. It was certainly a better option than letting someone else write their ending for them.

CHAPTER FIFTY-TWO

As Kanduu watched the living dummies file into position on his spire, he smiled to himself. It was almost time. He reached for a torch at the base of the structure, but his hand stilled when he heard a familiar voice behind him.

"Hello, old friend."

Kanduu spun around and came face-to-face with his old partner. The one who had trapped him inside Slappy. The one who had begun building the spire all those years ago. "Mahar?"

Mahar stepped forward, a slight smile on his face as he greeted the magician. "They brought me back," Mahar said, gesturing to Margot, James, Isabella, and Isaiah behind him.

"*He* stopped you before," Isaiah said. "*We* stopped you before. And now we're going to stop you together."

Kanduu turned to Mahar, the person who had betrayed him all those years ago. He shook his head in disbelief. Would his old friend really betray him *again*? "I gave you everything you wanted," Kanduu told him.

"You're right," Mahar said. Then he added, "I'm not here to stop you."

"What did he just say?" James whispered to Isabella.

Mahar stepped over to stand beside Kanduu. "What are you doing?" Margot gasped.

"Trying to fix the trust I broke a long time ago," Mahar said sadly. He grabbed the torch off the rail of the spire and stepped toward the opening that was stuffed full of kindling. "I'm sorry I was disloyal," Mahar said to Kanduu. "I didn't see it before, but now I do. You are a great genius, a man ahead of his time. And as I once promised before but failed to deliver on, I am your humble servant. I am here to help you bring the world back into balance once again. We must unleash the horrors!"

"It's good to see you, old friend," Kanduu said, delighted.

"Start the ritual," Mahar said. He stepped forward, pressing the torch toward the mouth of the spire.

As the fire took hold, Kanduu began his incantations. *"Nusku Rantok Krastani Meluu . . ."* The four teens watched in horror as the fire took hold and shot up the spire. Nora, Ben, Eliza, Victoria, Colin, their teachers . . . and Lucas. All engulfed in flames. "It is working, Mahar!" Kanduu cried as he stared up at the fire, enraptured. "We did it!"

But then, Kanduu's face began to harden and crack. His mouth formed into a dummy shape as he, too, became a puppet. Just as he realized what had happened, Mahar's face melted away and revealed Nathan standing in front of him instead, holding up a torch.

It was all a fantasy, playing out in Kanduu's mind. They'd taken the magician's own trick and turned it around on him. Nathan waved in front of Kanduu's Slappified face a few times to check that it had, indeed, worked. "He's still out!" he called, bringing the torch over to where the others were poring over Kanduu's field journal to try to find the spell that would reverse everything.

"Have you found the right incantation yet?" he asked. "It's 'Madonna' something. Then maybe an 's.' You just say it in reverse, and it breaks the spell."

"Are you sure?" James asked. Nathan hadn't exactly proven himself to be the most reliable guy when it came to most things.

As they flipped through the pages in the journal, the magic began to wear off on Kanduu. The trick had only lasted a few seconds. "That spell doesn't work on me," he told them, now fully alert and back to his human form again.

Isaiah grabbed the torch from Nathan and held it under Kanduu's field journal. "You stop right there!" he ordered. "Or I burn this journal and all your magic with it."

Kanduu smirked. "I know every word in that book. I've been studying it my whole life." Casually, he began to speak aloud another incantation. *"Nusku Rantok Krastani Meluu . . ."* Just as he finished his last word, the earth began to shake. Fissures erupted outward from the base of the spire, opening wider and wider until they were massive chasms. Dark vapors began to pour out of them like smoky tendrils, climbing up the spire filled with Slappified people.

His smile widening, Kanduu watched as the tendrils also wrapped around the four teens and Nathan, pulling them all to the ground, toward the open chasms. Kanduu stepped forward and grabbed another torch from the spire's core. It was time.

Isaiah continued to struggle against the smoke, desperate to do something, *anything* to help all the people he loved. He was still holding the field journal, and he noticed that the vapors seemed to be repulsed by the old leather diary. Isaiah swung the diary around, holding it up to the tendrils to press them back and free himself. Just as Kanduu was about to light the kindling at the base of the spire, Isaiah used the journal again to free Margot from the smoke's clutches. "Find a spell," he told her, handing over the book. "Reverse all this. I'll hold him."

Isaiah began to run. He dodged through the vapor tendrils like he was running past defenders on the football field. With a mighty leap, he dove into Kanduu, knocking the torch out of the magician's hand. The torch rolled as Isaiah pinned the magician down, but it kept rolling, getting closer and closer to the spire. Suddenly, it caught the wood at the edge of the platform base, and the flames crept ever closer to the kindling at the spire's core.

Just then, Margot found the spell she was pretty sure Nathan had been talking about. "This is it!" she cried. "Okay, okay. *Kanduu Azana Moori.* She looked up, hopeful, to where Isaiah and Kanduu had been wrestling for control near the spire.

Now she saw that Kanduu had suddenly gone still. He stared up at the spire and muttered, "No . . ."

Margot nodded. "I reversed the spell that saved your life," she told him. "And now everything you did is coming undone."

The magician looked up and saw that everyone on the spire had now become human again. People were beginning to scream, and they were all running to escape. It was over; his ritual was ruined before it could even truly begin.

And he, Kanduu, had turned suddenly back into Rupert. Back in his old battle uniform. Suddenly, he looked down at his stomach and saw that his old injury had returned, too. Blood was soaking through his clothing, and he was—once again—mortally wounded. But this time, there was no magic spell that could save him.

As people rushed to get away from the spire, Kanduu staggered toward it, wounded and screaming. "No!" he screamed, pain and anguish evident in his voice. "No! No!"

Suddenly, soldiers from the battle that had nearly taken his life all those years ago began to emerge from the chasms on the field. They charged at Kanduu, grabbing for him as he screamed in terror. "Get away from me!" he shrieked. Just then, the magician drew a pistol out of his uniform and held it out in front of him. He spun, turning to face Margot. "You!" he screamed, raising the weapon to point it straight at the person who had done this to him.

He cocked the gun and fired. Isaiah jumped before he could even think about what he was doing, diving in front of the bullet as it raced toward Margot. It struck Isaiah, knocking him sideways, and he stared into Margot's eyes as he rolled to the ground—Kanduu's final victim.

The soldiers continued their approach, rushing toward Kanduu as he screamed. Their hands grabbed for him, pulling him deep into the chasms that had split open the field. Just as soon as he was out of sight, the fissures in the ground closed up and disappeared. It was as though they—and Kanduu—had never been there at all.

But the damage he had inflicted was very real, including the bullet that had shot Isaiah. And that wound wasn't disappearing along with all the other magic.

"Isaiah!" his mom screamed, running straight from her own

nightmarish perch on the spire to the nightmare her son was still going through on the ground. Once again, he'd been hurt on the football field. But this time, it wasn't just a broken arm.

"Hang in there, buddy," Ben said as Isaiah's eyes drifted closed, blood leaking from his wound. "Hang in there!"

CHAPTER FIFTY-THREE

"This is all on us," Nora said as everyone hunkered down in the hospital waiting room late that night.

"No, Nora," Colin said, trying to comfort her. "It's not—"

"We should have stopped this," she said, crying. "We should have stopped this a long time ago, and instead, we passed it on to our kids. And now Isaiah is in there, paying the price."

"He did it for Margot," James told Lucas.

"I know," Lucas said sadly.

The ER doctor stepped out into the hallway and pulled Isaiah's parents aside. Margot crept close enough that she could hear what the doctor was saying. "This is never easy," the doctor said, taking a deep breath. "But I'm not sure what we can do for him other than make him comfortable."

"What are you saying?" Isaiah's mom asked, unable to comprehend the doctor's words. She turned to Ben. "What is she saying?" Ben shook his head, and Laura crumpled into his arms. Their son was dying? Death was the only outcome? Ben let his tears fall as he held his wife, and they cried together.

When no one was watching, Margot crept into Isaiah's hospital room. Her best friend's bed was surrounded by machines, all of them whirring and beeping and helping to keep him alive, since his own body couldn't do that for him anymore. She had to tell him everything she'd always wanted him to know. She had to say everything she had planned, and she had to do it fast. "This is what I didn't—couldn't—say to you before," she began. "Yes. Yes, Isaiah, I do want to be with you. I have always wanted to be with you. But I'm scared. Scared of ruining things. And losing you." She choked on her own tears, but forced herself to continue. "You always break my heart. In fact, it's kind of what you're best at—even now. But I would give anything to have you back. I would risk anything to have us back."

The machine by her side stopped beeping. Isaiah's heart had stopped. It was nearly over.

But Margot shook her head, pulling the field journal out of her jacket pocket. She had one last thing to say. And now was her final chance to say it. *"Moori Azana Kanduu,"* she said, repeating the spell Kanduu had used all those years ago to heal himself in the cave. Maybe, just maybe, it would work for Isaiah, too.

Isaiah's eyes snapped open. He sat up and the machine by his side began to beep once again.

In the bathroom, Nathan splashed water on his face. It had been a *day*, hell, a *month*. He glanced up at himself in the mirror, knowing he probably looked even worse than he felt. But in the reflection of the mirror, he didn't see his own weary face looking back at him. He saw the face of Kanduu. Nathan's eyes went wide as Kanduu smiled back at him. Nathan blinked, unable to believe it. With a big sigh, he closed his eyes and muttered, "Not again."

AFTER

— *Bye-Bye, Slappy* —

HELLO, NEW NIGHTMARE

EPILOGUE

The cast was finally off, and everyone was relieved to see Isaiah whole again. He'd come out of the hospital looking better than ever. His rapid recovery was unexpected. The doctors had originally told his parents that Kanduu's bullet had done him in, but then *bam!* Something had happened inside that hospital room to revive him, and now all was good, including his previously busted arm.

Even better, he and Margot had been testing the waters on their new relationship ever since he got out of the hospital. They were taking things slowly. There was still some stuff to deal with where Lucas was concerned, but the two old friends were exploring new territory— a spin on their relationship they never thought would really happen.

Ever since that insane night with the spire ritual on the football field (the *second* insane night on the field, as far as Isaiah was concerned), things had finally, slowly been returning to normal for all the people in Port Lawrence. Isaiah had even been working with Margot to study more, so he could get his grades up. It was starting to feel like maybe he could get into college someday . . . possibly *without* that football scholarship.

Isabella and James's friendship was growing stronger, too. The friends bonded as they worked through James's constant struggles figuring out his relationship with Sam, and Isabella's continuing frustration that she'd lost out on her chance with Isaiah—again. Their shared troubles with their problematic moms helped bring them together, too.

And Lucas was . . . Lucas. No one could tell what he was really thinking or feeling most of the time, but they knew he was still grappling with the pain of almost losing his mom, his regret about giving up his shot with Margot, and the ongoing grief from losing his dad. Not to mention what he'd gone through when he'd been Slappified and almost burned to a crisp. Luckily, he had the new friends he'd bonded with during all the Biddle-Bratt drama, so at least he wasn't going through all this hard stuff totally alone.

Everyone had been busy trying to get their lives back to normal after all that had happened with Kanduu, Harold's ghost, Slappy, the haunted scrapbook, the possessed worms, the time-looping cuckoo clock, the haunted mask, and the evil camera. And now, *finally*, life was slowly returning to the usual boring Port Lawrence day-to-day. Which was good, since the long-awaited school trip to London had finally arrived, and there were big things in store for everyone.

Nathan had given up his job as English teacher at PLHS once his book deal had finally come through. Some critics claimed his book was derivative, but his editor had been thrilled with the new ending. Since he was on tour for his new book in London, he reached out to see if he could meet up with his former students across the pond.

He thought it would be nice to see some familiar faces, especially since he rarely got to see his own anymore. Plus, after everything they'd all gone through, it might be healing to spend time with some of the few people who knew what *actually* happened back in Port Lawrence.

Or, at least, *most* of what had happened. Nathan hadn't told anyone that he had been living a double life ever since that night on the football field. It turned out Kanduu wasn't quite as gone as it originally seemed. When the ghosts of fallen soldiers had dragged him into the depths of the earth, they'd left part of him behind—in Nathan.

Yet again, Kanduu and Nathan were sharing space in the same body. Nathan was never truly alone anymore. And it was starting to seem that Nathan's luck would *never* let him live alone again.

Isaiah was excited for the trip to London and to get away from Port Lawrence and all the bad memories that lingered there, at least for a while. Though he hadn't confessed this to anyone, ever since his miraculous recovery from Kanduu's 150-year-old bullet, nearly falling off a snowy cliff, and breaking his arm, Isaiah had been feeling . . . weird. He felt on edge all the time. He had strange dreams every night, and his appetite was insatiable, even more so than usual. Which was nuts, since when he was busy training, his appetite was always out of control.

Isaiah could tell Margot and his parents were worried about him. Margot, especially, had been keeping an extra close eye on him. *Did she know something he didn't*, he wondered? But he assured everyone he was fine, that it was just lingering trauma and he'd be back to his old self in time. For a while, Isaiah had even convinced himself things were looking up. Hopefully the escape to London would be a chance to finally complete the healing process.

As they boarded the plane for London, Isaiah found himself mostly worried about the long flight being awkward. He was sitting between Margot and Isabella, after all. But they were all friends. It wouldn't be *that* weird, right? Nothing he couldn't handle.

The plane was somewhere near Greenland when Isaiah started to feel *strange*. It wasn't too-many-Cokes-in-a-row-on-an-overnight-flight weird or nerves from being stuck between two girls he may or may not have feelings for. Nah, this was something else altogether. He hadn't felt anything like this since the night he'd woken up in the hospital, with the inexplicably healed gunshot wound and unbroken arm. Like he—or something else—was crawling out of his skin. Not literally, like Lucas's worms, but as though his whole body was trying to explode from within.

"What's going on with him?" Isabella hissed while Isaiah howled quietly in the seat beside her, clearly in some kind of pain.

Margot chewed her lip. Isaiah was scraping his fingernails along his thighs, shredding holes in the fabric of his pants. And when he glanced her way, his eyes were wild and practically glowing in the cabin of the dim plane.

Margot began to speak to Isaiah in the secret language they

made up as kids, hoping she could distract him from whatever nightmare was playing out in his body. But it was like he was somewhere else. Nothing she could say or do got through to him.

Isabella and Margot kept trying to distract Isaiah from whatever was happening in his body, but nothing they did calmed him down completely. By the time the plane was circling above Heathrow Airport, it had become increasingly obvious that they were just delaying the inevitable. Something was happening to their friend—some kind of change that was transforming him into someone wild and unfamiliar—and it was obviously going to happen soon.

They had barely reached the gate when their friend bolted to the front of the plane and was the first to disembark.

"Where is he going?" Margot asked Isabella. They were trapped near the back of the plane, waiting their turn to exit.

Isabella just shrugged. Shouldn't Margot know? She was supposedly his girlfriend now, after all. "Let's get our bags. Maybe he just really had to pee."

After they grabbed their luggage and went through customs, Margot and Isabella still hadn't found Isaiah. They both tried texting him, but got no response.

Margot looked worried. But as far as Isabella was concerned, Margot *always* looked worried. She was always obsessing over something. That's probably why Isaiah took off. He was sick of Margot's drama after ten hours in the air. A girl could hope he was sick of her, anyway. "I'm sure he just forgot to take his phone off airplane mode," she said, pulling Margot toward the ground transportation area. "Come on, we can meet up with him later. He's a big boy. I'm sure he can find his own way. I'm exhausted. Let's sleep off our jet lag so we can get our London on!"

By the next afternoon, James was already fully immersed in London life and enjoying the best it had to offer, in true James fashion. He'd hit up a bunch of shops that morning, grabbed high tea at a cute café with Isabella, and snapped a ton of amazing selfies next to the Tower Bridge to send back to Sam. He was hoping his absence would make Sam's heart grow even fonder, but a few pictures to remind Sam to miss him couldn't hurt, either.

Now he and Isabella were spending the afternoon exploring while Margot got all the details set for the British Museum mini-internship she'd arranged for their time in London.

"Did you talk to Isaiah last night?" Isabella asked with a yawn as she and James popped off the Tube and headed through Trafalgar Square, en route to pick up Lucas at the restaurant he was working at during their trip. He claimed it would be good experience for running the Harbor Stop someday (and a good way to make some money for all his hobbies), but James was convinced a job was nothing more than a way to ruin a perfectly good vacation.

"No," James said. "I went to bed early. Jet lag is no joke."

Isabella frowned. Had *anyone* seen Isaiah since he bolted off the plane yesterday afternoon? He was supposed to be figuring out what he needed to do before he started the sporty-boy football intensive thing his coach had set up for him, so it wasn't weird she hadn't seen him yet today. And even though she hadn't gotten a text from him, either, she figured Margot probably had. It wasn't like he *had* to text her. Still, it would be nice to hear *something* from him after he'd been acting so weird on the plane the whole flight over.

She stopped short in front of a dingy-looking restaurant-pub thing and peered through the window. "Is this the place?" she asked James.

As if in answer to her question, Lucas stepped out the restaurant's front door, onto the sidewalk. He looked like he'd just rolled out of bed, as always. "Hey," he said with a slight wave.

"How's our working man?" James said with a smirk.

"Cash is king," Lucas replied. He shuffled away from his London job, seething about the fact that *some* people didn't need jobs. *Some* people got money handed to them on a silver platter. He glanced at James and added, "Which I'm sure you know well enough."

"Touché!" James said with a grin.

"Which way are we going? This way, right?" Isabella asked, looking at street signs for a clue. She glanced left to check for traffic, then stepped into the street to cross. A car honked and its tires squealed before swerving to miss her.

"They drive on the other side of the road here," James pointed out helpfully, just a few moments too late.

Isabella's heart was racing. That was a close one. She was definitely going to need to be more alert in London. After all the close calls she'd had over the past few months with Slappy and Kanduu and Harold and the possessed mask, she was very much wishing for a much less dramatic and heart-pounding time in London.

Unfortunately, wishes rarely came true.

"We're meeting everyone at the corner of something and something," James said, pulling out his phone to check details in the group text.

"It's this way," Lucas said, leading them through the streets of London to where they were supposed to be meeting up with Isaiah and Margot before they all went to visit Mr. Bratt. None of them were particularly excited to see their old teacher, but he had begged to connect with them in London. They still felt bad for everything the guy had gone through since moving into the old Biddle house—and he offered to pay for dinner with his book advance money—so they'd agreed.

When they got to their meetup spot, Margot was already there. But she was alone.

"Where's Isaiah?" James asked.

"I don't know," Margot said, sounding confused. "I've been at the museum all morning. You guys haven't heard anything from him?"

Before anyone could answer, Isaiah came rushing toward them from the opposite direction. His eyes were bloodshot, and his short hair was unusually unkempt. It looked like he'd been up all night. His hands were shaking, and there was dirt under his fingernails. And as he pulled his sleeves down, Margot noticed long scratches covering his forearms. "Dude, you don't look good," Lucas said. "Not enough sleep?"

"Something like that," Isaiah said, shaking his head. "Just a weird night."

James, Isabella, and Lucas set off down the sidewalk, but

Margot hung back beside Isaiah. She wanted to get some distance from the others before asking, "Where'd you go after the airport? And why haven't you texted? We were all really worried about you."

"I got lost and my phone was dead," he responded, but Margot could tell he wasn't giving her the whole story. "I'm sorry, Margot. It's just—" He wouldn't meet her eyes, and there was something off about him—something twitchy—that made her wonder what he wasn't telling her. And that same wonder made her worry. What was going on with him?

She reached for his hand as they walked through London's streets to meet Mr. Bratt. But before she could touch him, Isaiah pulled away, acting like he was going to grab his phone. He smiled at her apologetically, but Margot frowned. He was avoiding touching her. Why?

Isaiah had been acting off ever since the night of Kanduu's spire on the football field. She'd thought it was just the trauma of everything that had happened to him at first—almost dying probably takes a real toll—and that it would get better with time. But it hadn't gotten better. In fact, things seemed to be getting worse. And Margot was worried this was partly her fault: Had something happened when she'd said that spell in his hospital room? Might she have somehow accidentally unlocked some new horror in her effort to save Isaiah's life?

They'd come to England for a much-needed break, but Margot suddenly had a very bad feeling that the horrors that had haunted the five of them in Port Lawrence definitely weren't over. Instead, a whole new nightmare had followed them to London.